THE GAUNTLET

Down came the lances to the charge, and the two men pounded over the soft turf, the hooves of their chargers throwing up big clods of grass. The sun flashed in hard gleams on the tips of the highly polished helmets . . . They met with a crash, and a crack of lances.

When Peter finds the gauntlet on a Welsh hillside, he becomes the latest link in an old legend. Suddenly transported back to the fourteenth century, to a world of castles, feasts, jousts, and battles, he is accepted by everyone as the eldest son of Sir Roger de Blois. Peter learns how to live as the son of a Norman lord, how to hawk, and fight, and shoot a longbow, and, finally, he has to escape from their besieged castle to bring help. But one day he will have to return to his own time . . .

Ronald Welch (Ronald Oliver Felton) was born in Glamorgan and for much of his life was a teacher of history, and Headmaster of Okehampton Grammar School. He fought in the Welch Regiment during World War II. He published a number of historical novels for children, including *Knight Crusader* in 1954, for which he won the Carnegie Medal.

D1393412

Other Oxford Children's Modern Classics

The Eagle of the Ninth
Rosemary Sutcliff

Outcast
Rosemary Sutcliff

The Silver Branch
Rosemary Sutcliff

The Lantern Bearers
Rosemary Sutcliff

Minnow on the Say
Philippa Pearce

Tom's Midnight Garden
Philippa Pearce

The Ship That Flew
Hilda Lewis

A Little Lower than the Angels
Geraldine McCaughrean

A Pack of Lies
Geraldine McCaughrean

Brother in the Land
Robert Swindells

Flambards
K. M. Peyton

The Edge of the Cloud
K. M. Peyton

Flambards in Summer
K. M. Peyton

Flambards Divided
K. M. Peyton

Wolf
Gillian Cross

The Great Elephant Chase
Gillian Cross

The Hounds of the Morrigan
Pat O'Shea

RONALD WELCH

The Gauntlet

Illustrated by

T. R. FREEMAN

OXFORD
UNIVERSITY PRESS

OXFORD

UNIVERSITY PRESS

Great Clarendon Street, Oxford OX2 6DP

Oxford University Press is a department of the University of Oxford.
It furthers the University's objective of excellence in research, scholarship,
and education by publishing worldwide in

Oxford New York

Athens Auckland Bangkok Bogotá Buenos Aires Calcutta
Cape Town Chennai Dar es Salaam Delhi Florence Hong Kong Istanbul
Karachi Kuala Lumpur Madrid Melbourne Mexico City Mumbai
Nairobi Paris São Paulo Singapore Taipei Tokyo Toronto Warsaw

and associated companies in Berlin Ibadan

Oxford is a registered trade mark of Oxford University Press
in the UK and in certain other countries

Copyright © Ronald Welch 1951

The moral rights of the author have been asserted

First published 1951
First published in this edition 1999
Reprinted 1999

All rights reserved. No part of this publication may be reproduced,
stored in a retrieval system, or transmitted, in any form or by any means,
without the prior permission in writing of Oxford University Press.
Within the UK, exceptions are allowed in respect of any fair
dealing for the purpose of research or private study, or criticism or
review, as permitted under the Copyright, Designs and Patents Act 1988,
or in the case of reprographic reproduction in accordance with
the terms of the licences issued by the Copyright Licensing Agency.
Enquiries concerning reproduction outside these terms and in other
countries should be sent to the Rights Department, Oxford University Press,
at the above address.

This book is sold subject to the condition that it shall not, by way of trade or
otherwise, be lent, re-sold, hired out or otherwise circulated without
the publisher's prior consent in any form of binding or cover other than that in
which it is published and without a similar condition including this condition
being imposed on the subsequent purchaser.

British Library Cataloguing in Publication Data available

Cover illustration by Barry Jones

ISBN 0 19 271762 6

Printed in Great Britain

FOR

Mary and Mayzod

AUTHOR'S NOTE

Some of the names of people and places in this story are imaginary, whilst others are taken from history.

There is, for instance, a castle at Carreg Cennen (sometimes spelt Caer Cynan on maps), about five miles from Llandilo. It is still in a good state of preservation, including the extraordinary passage cut through the solid rock of the precipice. Kidwelly Castle is now in the hands of Cadw, the Welsh Historic Monuments division of National Heritage, who have preserved the whole castle.

There was a monastery at Valle Crucis, but it is in North Wales, and not where I have placed it in this book. The names of the South Wales Marcher Lords are historic, except for the family of de Blois, and there is no such village as Llanferon.

CONTENTS

LIST OF ILLUSTRATIONS

1

Peter Finds the Gauntlet

'I'm sure we're going the wrong way,' Peter Staunton said. 'Let's try to the left for a change.'

'No! Straight on!' Gwyn Evans retorted with great confidence.

Peter shrugged his shoulders, and stumbled over the uneven ground behind Gwyn. The mountain mist had closed down on them now, thick, damp and clinging, with an air of grim persistence that was somewhat alarming.

They were quite hopelessly lost, Peter decided, and had been so for the last half-hour, ever since they had wandered off the narrow sheep-track along which they had made their way across the top of the mountain. It was this track they were trying to find now, for without its help they had not the slightest idea of even the direction they should take. If they found it, they were as good as home. If not . . . but Peter shied away from the thought.

He stumbled and nearly fell. Gwyn heard his sudden exclamation, and turned quickly.

'Found it?' he called out anxiously.

'No, worse luck. Tripped over something.'

Peter was bending down examining some object on the ground when Gwyn reached him.

'What on earth is it?' Gwyn asked.

'Haven't the foggiest,' Peter grunted. He picked up the object. 'Hi, wait a sec, Gwyn,' he said, as his friend started to move away. 'It looks interesting.'

'Waste of time, Peter. It's only an old glove.'

1

'Pretty funny one,' Peter remarked. 'It's made of iron. Look!'

Gwyn turned back reluctantly, and then his interest was aroused.

'Like a huge batting glove,' he said.

He was right, but it was larger and heavier than any cricket glove they had seen before. The inside of the glove covering the palm of the hand was of thick rough leather, worn and creased; the back of each finger and the thumb piece were covered with thick pieces of steel.

Peter gazed at it in silence. His head was feeling oddly numb, and the mist seemed to swirl around him with redoubled speed and thickness. Hardly realizing what he was doing, he slipped his right hand inside the heavy gauntlet, and his fingers groped inside the wide spaces, for it was far too large for his small hand.

From behind there came the thud of hooves, a shout, shrill and defiant, the clang of metal on metal, and then a confused roar of sounds, shouts, more hoof-beats, clang after clang, dying away into the distance as suddenly as they had come. The gauntlet slipped from Peter's hand, and he shook himself as if he had just awakened.

'What was that?' he whispered.

'What?' asked Gwyn looking curiously at Peter's face.

'Horses, and somebody shouting,' Peter said, shaking his head to try and clear away the sensation of numbness.

'Horses!' Gwyn peered into the white mist that surrounded them. 'I didn't hear anything. Might be a farmer. That means we're close to the track. Come on, Peter!'

He dashed off, and as his figure disappeared in the clinging mist, Peter shook his head once more, and hurried after him. Almost immediately he heard a triumphant shout from Gwyn.

'Here it is, Peter. The track!'

Peter laughed with sudden relief, and the odd sensation of numbness and dread which had swept over him disappeared in a flash, as he reached Gwyn's side. They were standing on a thin track that wound its way like a snake over the rough ground. Unimpressive as it appeared, that thin line meant home, tea, and a roaring fire.

'Which way though?' he said.

'We must work this out scientifically,' Gwyn said.

Peter grinned. He had heard Gwyn before on scientific methods.

'No need,' he said. 'See that bush there? That was on our right when we came up, so if we keep it on the left now, we'll go the right way.'

'How do you know it's the same bush?' snapped Gwyn.

'Sure of it,' Peter said doggedly. 'I remember the pile of stones on one side.'

'OK,' Gwyn said, 'I remember now. That's what I mean by working it out scientifically.'

'Sez you,' Peter retorted rudely, and set off briskly along the track.

Now that they had found the track, they wasted little time, and kept up a good pace. Ten minutes hard walking brought them to the foot of the mountain. The lower they dropped, the more the mist lifted, until they suddenly found themselves in the bright sunshine of mid-afternoon.

'Ought to see Carreg Cennen now,' Gwyn said.

'What's that?' Peter asked quickly. He had never heard the name before, he felt certain, but there was a curious feeling of familiarity about it that aroused his interest.

'It's a castle,' Gwyn said, 'over in that direction,' and he pointed to the left.

They were at the foot of the mountain now, about a mile further up the valley from their original starting-point earlier that afternoon. Peter looked in the direction of Gwyn's finger, and saw the ground rise sharply to a narrow point. It was difficult to see how high it was, for the mist still covered at least half the slope. But over the top of the white mist Peter saw the turrets of a ruined castle. They looked grim and forbidding in that lonely spot, and had an air of brooding watchfulness.

'Gosh! That's marvellous!' Peter muttered.

'Not bad,' Gwyn said indifferently. He had seen Carreg Cennen before, and castles, as he had told Peter several times, were not in his line. Not scientific enough.

But to Peter that brief glimpse had meant a great deal. For history fascinated him, not only the actual reading, but the sight of old buildings, spots where battles had been fought, any place where his vivid imagination was given an opportunity of conjuring up the past. And Carreg Cennen had caught his interest in a way he had never experienced before. As he followed Gwyn down the winding road, his eyes kept switching round as if drawn by some giant magnet. Then they turned a corner, and the turrets dropped from sight.

They were home half an hour later, for Peter was staying with an uncle of Gwyn's, a Mr Evans, who lived in a large sprawling house in the depths of the Welsh mountains, and just outside the village of Llanferon. Tea was ready for them in the lounge, a long room at the front of the house, and Mr Evans himself, a short alert little Welshman, was pouring out.

'Expecting the vicar,' he said. 'He often drops in about this time.'

Peter and Gwyn started to eat, for they were hungry after their climb. This was one of the best moments of the day, Peter decided, as he ploughed his way steadily through a plateful of crumpets, and glanced round the walls of the room, with the high bookcases, and rows of books.

'Ah, here he is,' Mr Evans said, as voices were heard in the hall outside.

The Vicar of Llanferon was a pleasant sight, tall, stout, and with a round red face of great cheerfulness. His hair was white, but his manner was that of a much younger man, with tremendous enthusiasm and vigour.

'What have you two been doing with yourselves?' he asked, after he had filled his plate with crumpets.

'We went up Carn Eglwys, sir,' Gwyn said.

'Ah, interesting spot that,' the vicar said. 'They call it the Hill of the Normans around here, you know.'

'That's a queer name, sir,' Peter said, his historical sense aroused. 'Is there any special reason?'

'Oh, yes,' the vicar said, turning towards Peter and obviously pleased at finding someone interested in his own pet subject of local history. 'There was a battle fought up there. Back in the eleventh century. The Normans were in the process of overrunning South Wales then, you see, and the Welsh in this area made a last stand on the mountain.'

'Who won?' Gwyn said.

'Difficult to say, my dear boy. It was a pretty murderous fight, by all accounts, and the mist made it even . . . '

'The mist?' Peter said quickly.

'Yes. There was a heavy mist on the mountain, according to the old chronicle, the sort of weather you ran into this afternoon, and both sides had a good many casualties. The Welsh withdrew into the valleys, so I suppose you might call it a Norman victory.'

'Welsh!' Gwyn said stoutly.

'Norman!' Peter insisted.

They grinned at each other, and the vicar watched them with a smile. For there was a curious racial difference about their appearance; Peter with his dark hair and straight clear-cut features; and Gwyn, dark too, but with the slightly olive complexion of the pure Welsh strain. They were both of them startling throwbacks to the two races from which they had sprung.

Peter's imagination had already started to picture the scene on Carn Eglwys, the white drifting mist, the half-seen figures on horseback, the shouts, the clang of swords, the drum of hooves on the soft turf . . .

He sat up with a jerk.

'The gauntlet!' he exclaimed sharply. 'The gauntlet!'

'The what?' gasped the vicar. He dropped his pipe with a clatter in the stone fireplace, and leant forward, staring at Peter with an expression of the most extraordinary intentness. Mr Evans, too, was watching with a similar glance of sudden excited interest.

'I found a funny sort of glove on the mountain,' Peter said.

'Yes, so we did,' Gwyn added. 'Like a batting glove, except that it had thick chunks of iron on the back instead of rubber.'

'Did you put it on, Peter?' the vicar said eagerly.

'Yes, I did,' Peter said, and the vicar grunted softly, his eyes still fixed intently on Peter's face.

'Did you see or hear anything?' Mr Evans asked.

'Yes, I did,' Peter said slowly, trying to remember what had happened. 'I heard horses galloping, some shouts, and what sounded like loud clangs, as if there was a fight going on with swords and armour.'

'Aaah!' breathed the vicar. He sank back into his chair, and exchanged glances with Mr Evans. The two old gentlemen nodded at each other.

'"There are more things in Heaven and Earth,"' muttered the vicar under his breath.

But Peter had caught the remark, and he recognized the quotation from *Hamlet*. He sat up quickly.

'What do you mean, sir?' he asked curiously.

'There's a curious legend about Carn Eglwys,' the vicar said.

'About the battle?' Peter asked.

'Yes. At a certain time of the year, people have found a medieval gauntlet up there, and then heard sounds of battle. Shouts, the thud of hooves, the clash of swords.'

'What?' Peter said. He rubbed his forehead in bewildered excitement.

'Just as you did,' Mr Evans said. 'Around Easter. The battle was fought on Easter Monday, you see.'

'Have you ever found the gauntlet?' Peter asked.

The two men shook their heads regretfully.

'Never,' the vicar said. 'And not for lack of trying.'

'But who has heard these sounds?' Peter persisted.

'Well, old Rice Llewellyn, for one,' the vicar said. 'He lives in Llanferon. He says he saw figures, besides hearing the sounds. They were on horseback, and carrying shields.'

'Imagination,' Gwyn said.

'Oh, no, my dear Gwyn,' the vicar said emphatically. He drew fiercely on his pipe, and blew a great cloud of blue smoke across the room. 'There was the evidence of the shields. That was conclusive. Conclusive!' he boomed triumphantly.

'But why?'

'Old Rice described the shields. He said they were kite shaped,' Mr Evans said in his soft Welsh voice.

'And the Norman shields *were* kite shaped!' exclaimed the vicar. 'You can see them on the Bayeaux Tapestry.'

He leant forward in his chair, and pointed the stem of his pipe at Peter.

'And how could he know that?' he demanded excitedly. 'Old Rice never went to school. He can't even read, and I don't suppose he has ever opened a book in his life!'

Even Gwyn whistled softly at that evidence, whilst Peter wriggled in his chair with excitement and mounting interest.

There was silence in the room, and they all stared at the fire. A log dropped, and a shower of sparks shot up, followed by a spurt of flame.

'What about the other people who found the gauntlet?' Peter asked after a pause.

'Ah!' The vicar sat up again. 'Now, that's very interesting. John,' and he waved the pipe in the direction of Mr Evans, 'John and I made a close study of that part of the legend. There was Lord Roust, in Queen Anne's day. He had estates near Llanferon.'

'There was Roger Williams in 1640,' Mr Evans said.

'And Mervyn Rees in 1802.'

'David Llewelly in 1858.'

'And, of course, the Frenchman, in 1870!' the vicar said with an air of a man producing his trump card. 'That proved our point, John. Proved my theory to the hilt!'

'What is your theory, sir?' Peter asked.

'Ah, now you're asking, my dear boy!' The vicar was full of his absorbing hobby now. 'One fact struck us immediately about this story. We noticed in every case that the person who found the gauntlet had some long-standing connection with Carn Eglwys. Lord Roust, for instance, was a direct descendant of a Norman baron who settled here at that time. Probably fought in the actual battle.'

'But the villagers?' Peter asked. 'What about Rice Llewellyn?'

'That's the beauty of it,' the vicar said with delight. 'In an isolated village like Llanferon whole families have lived in the same spot for generations. Look at the old parish records, for instance.'

Peter nodded. He was quite prepared to look at the parish records, and he was just about to say so. But the vicar was in full flood now.

'Now you must admit,' he went on briskly, 'that it is quite feasible that old Rice, for instance, is descended from one of those very Welshmen who fought on Carn Eglwys. And the same applies to the other Llanferon people who found the gauntlet. Even more probable in their case. That's incontrovertible,' the vicar said defiantly, as if he were expecting Peter to argue the point. 'Incontrovertible!' he repeated, rolling the great syllables round his tongue with relish.

Peter nodded silently. He had no wish to argue. He was perfectly willing to believe the whole theory; it was far too fascinating, quite apart from the fact that he had not the slightest notion of the meaning of incontrovertible.

But Gwyn was more critical.

'But the Frenchman, sir,' he said. 'He had nothing to do with Llanferon.'

The vicar swung round, his face alight with triumph. This, Peter felt, was a thrill, the real ace of trumps, the one fact that would prove the whole fascinating story.

'Aha, that's just where you're wrong, Gwyn!' the vicar said. 'That Frenchman's name was Jean de Crespigny. Now,' and he paused dramatically, 'one of the Norman knights who fought up there was a certain Raoul de Crespigny!' He sank back into his chair. 'You see, conclusive! Conclusive!'

It was indeed, and Peter nodded with delight. His brain was filled with wonderful pictures of castle walls, flying pennons, the excited whinny of horses, the bright sheen of armour, and the triumphant flash of sword and shield.

Mr Evans stirred in his chair, and broke the silence.

'But you have forgotten one fact,' he said quietly to the vicar. 'And it completely explodes your theory.'

The vicar sat up with a jerk.

'Explodes it, John?' he said. 'What on earth do you mean?'

'You've forgotten that Peter found the gauntlet today. And he has never been to Llanferon before. He has no possible connection with Wales, or with Normandy, or with Carn Eglwys!'

The vicar stared at Peter in dismay, and his mouth opened in horror.

'Of course,' he muttered. 'Dear me, John, this is a disaster. You're quite right. It does explode my theory.'

He twisted his pipe in his long fingers, and stared miserably at the glowing heart of the fire.

Then Peter broke the silence.

'But I may have a connection,' he said.

'What connection, my dear boy?' The vicar turned to him eagerly.

'I'm half French, sir,' Peter said.

'Why, of course you are!' Gwyn exclaimed. 'Your mother is French, isn't she? She was left that marvellous *château* in Normandy last year.'

'Normandy!' exclaimed the vicar in rising excitement. 'Now, quick, Peter! What was your mother's name before she was married, and where is the *château*?'

'It's near Bayeux,' Peter said. 'She was left it by her grandfather, the Count de Blois.'

'De Blois!' shouted the vicar.

His face was shining with excitement, and he wheeled round in his chair, and gestured at Mr Evans, who smiled back in response.

'There you are, John!' the vicar said. 'The final conclusive clue! That settles it.'

'But why?' Peter asked.

The vicar beamed at him in delight.

'The leader of the Normans on Carn Eglwys,' he said, 'was Gaston de Blois. It was he who built Carreg Cennen Castle!'

2

Carreg Cennen Castle

It was not until after half-past eight that Peter awoke the next morning, and he might have slept even longer if he had not been disturbed by the loud rattle of his window. He rolled over, and sat up. Occasional gusts of rain were driving in through the open window, and with a groan, Peter left his warm bed, and ran across.

It was anything but a pleasant sight outside. Heavy curtains of rain were driving in continuously from the mountains, and then hurling themselves against the old house. The mountains were wreathed in heavy white mist, and Peter shivered in the cold draughts.

He dressed slowly, and wondered what they could do for the rest of the day. The vicar had pleaded urgent parish business soon after they had discovered that Peter was a descendant of the de Blois family, but they had arranged that he should meet the two boys at Carreg Cennen Castle after lunch. But there seemed little hope of that now. The rain looked as if it was set for the day.

Eventually Peter and Gwyn spent the morning in the lounge. Gwyn was fully occupied with his stamps, whilst Peter buried himself in some of Mr Evans's books.

By lunch-time he knew a good deal of the history of the Welsh side of the de Blois family. The first of them, the Gaston de Blois who had fought on the mountain, had carved out a large estate for himself, and it had remained in the family until the last of the male de Blois had been killed on the battlefield of Poitiers. The lands had then

12

passed to Lord Roust whose descendants still owned the
ruins of Carreg Cennen.

The vicar put in an appearance soon after eleven, and he
picked up the book Peter was reading.

'Castles,' he said. 'I think John and I have been over
practically every castle in the country.'

But Peter was not listening.

'I say, sir,' he said. 'Don't you think it would be a good
idea if Gwyn and I went up Carn Eglwys on Easter
Monday?'

'What?' The vicar dropped the book, and stared at Peter
in alarm. He rubbed his chin, and then shook his head.
'Better not, Peter,' he said. 'Better not.'

'But there's nothing wrong with it, is there?' Peter asked
with some surprise.

'Oh, no, of course not,' the vicar said hastily. 'But there
are some things best left alone, you know, my dear boy.'

'There's not a soul in Llanferon who would go up there
on Easter Monday,' Mr Evans said.

Peter dropped the subject, but the more he thought
about it, the more he was determined to climb Carn
Eglwys on the following Monday. But he wisely kept this
to himself, and joined Gwyn in making arrangements to
meet the vicar at the castle after lunch.

The rain cleared during lunch, and they reached the
castle soon after two. It was not a long walk, but a slow
one. They followed the main road, and then went through
a gate and across a field. A rough track led across the field,
and then climbed steeply to the gatehouse of the castle.
Carreg Cennen was not a large building, and could not
have been so before it fell into ruins. There was a round
tower at each corner, a line of grey crumbling walls, and a
small gatehouse, with small towers on either side. But
there was still a good deal standing, so there would be
plenty to see, Peter thought.

As they climbed the steep path, Peter began to realize that Carreg Cennen, despite its smallness, was a remarkable castle. He had heard the vicar describe it as 'the most romantic castle in the country', and he suddenly discovered why. For it was the position of the castle that made it such an amazing building. From where Peter stood now, he could see one solitary farmhouse. The village of Llanferon was around the corner of the road, and out of sight. There was nothing to be seen except the bare slopes of the mountains, the thin winding road which was seldom used by modern traffic, and then more hills again. Carreg Cennen was the most isolated castle in Wales. The view, Peter realized with a thrill, could not be very different from that which Gaston de Blois would have seen had he stopped his horse at the spot where Peter and Gwyn stood now.

Peter sat down on the short clipped grass at the foot of the gatehouse, and waited for the vicar. Gwyn was impatient. But Peter was in his element. His imagination could have full play here. Many times he had visited old buildings, and try as he could, he had found it difficult to visualize the scene he wished, for modern towns and buildings had crept up on the walls and windows of most medieval castles and cathedrals. But *here*!

He looked up at the ruined and crumbling gatehouse. If a sentry of 1200 had peered over the wall then, he would have seen the same scene for as far as the eye could reach. Peter wriggled with delight.

'Here he is!' Gwyn said suddenly, and Peter reluctantly came back to the twentieth century.

Coming up the road was an aged car, its engine protesting loudly at the hard work it was being called upon to perform. With a honk on the horn, the vicar thrust out his right hand, and swerved violently across the road, heading towards the open gate.

'He's going to hit it!' exclaimed Gwyn.

He was right. There was quite a good deal of room, but even that was not enough for the vicar. He charged through the gate like a tank, and the off-rear mudguard scraped the edge of the gate. But the vicar was quite unruffled. Without bothering to stop, he swung to the left, and lurched to a halt.

He was climbing out as the boys approached.

'You hit your mudguard, sir,' Peter said.

'That's nothing, Peter,' the vicar said cheerfully. 'I often do that. No harm done, you see,' he said, and turned to look up at the castle.

'There you are, Peter,' he boomed, waving one hand in the air with a magnificent gesture. 'The home of your ancestors! A positive eagle's nest!' The expression evidently caught his fancy, for he repeated it with great gusto, and in tones that echoed round the field. 'An eagle's nest! Yes, that's exactly what it is.'

He led them briskly through the ruined entrance, and into the main courtyard. There was little to be seen there, for the various buildings that had once stood against the massive outer walls had all gone. There were a few piles of boulders, a line of grey stones to mark the original foundations, but nothing more.

'Here we are,' the vicar announced. 'You can see the general lay-out from here. Know anything about castles, either of you?'

Gwyn shook his head. Peter had no chance to do even that, for it was quite clear that the vicar would have taken no notice if one of them had stated that he was an expert on the subject. He was well away on the topic of his favourite hobby, and wild horses would not have silenced him now.

'Right!' he said with tremendous satisfaction. 'We'll start with the Normans then . . . ' and he was off.

Gwyn sat down on the nearest pile of stones, and Peter, after a few seconds, when he realized that the vicar was likely to carry on for the next ten minutes, followed his example. But whereas Gwyn listened with half his attention only, Peter tried to take in the lecture. But even his enthusiasm was soon swamped by the vicar's eloquence.

For the old gentleman knew his subject. He took them faithfully through all the stages of castle building, from the simple castle of the Normans to the vast and elaborate fortresses of Edward the First. He spared them no technical term; many-syllabled and mysterious words such as motte and bailey, curtain walls, machicolation, barbicans, drum towers, and concentric lines of defence, flew past the bewildered ears of his audience, and rebounded from the great walls behind them.

'Perfectly simple, you see,' he said at last. 'A gradual and logical evolution from the motte and bailey to the concentric fortress of Caerphilly and Beaumaris. Now, have you got that all quite clearly in your heads?'

He rounded on his audience.

'Er . . . yes, quite clear, thank you, vicar,' Gwyn said hastily. He had understood one word in ten, but he had enough sense to realize that if he said anything else, he would merely reopen the flood of eloquence again.

'Good!' the vicar said. 'Now, come up here, and you'll see something really worth seeing.'

He climbed a half-ruined flight of stairs, and they followed him to the top of the ruined battlements. Peter leant over, shut his eyes quickly and recoiled in horror.

'Pretty good, eh?' boomed the vicar.

It was more than that. It was astounding. For below was a sheer precipitous drop of three hundred feet. And Peter suddenly realized what the vicar had meant by the expression 'eagle's nest'.

Carreg Cennen was built on the edge of a great cliff that rose abruptly from the valley. Only one side, that which faced the road, was a gradual rise; the other sides were formed by that terrifying cliff-face.

Peter gasped, and turned round to look at the gatehouse. Why, he thought, they need not have bothered to build any walls at all on three sides; nobody could possibly have climbed that appalling cliff.

'Now, come down here,' the vicar exclaimed. 'This is unique. Nothing like it in any other castle in the kingdom.'

They followed him down the stairs, across the courtyard, and through a low doorway of stone. Peter found it difficult to believe that there could be anything more astonishing at Carreg Cennen than the cliff, but he was mistaken.

He found himself in a narrow low-roofed tunnel, cut out of the solid rock of the cliff. Narrow loop-holes had been hacked on one side to light the tunnel.

'What on earth is this, sir?' he asked. 'A secret way out of the castle?'

'Oh, no, nothing as romantic as that,' the vicar said. 'It's the way to the well and cistern. There it is, you can see it quite distinctly. Filled up and blocked long ago, of course, but there's no doubt about it.'

There was, indeed, no doubt. They could see the wide gaping depression in the floor where the water supply had come from, so necessary to a castle which might have to stand a siege of months without relief.

They spent another half-hour exploring the castle, but there was not a great deal more to be seen. For the wear and tear of centuries had reduced Carreg Cennen to a vast shell; the great curtain walls still towered over the valley, but the interior of the building had vanished, with but faint traces to show where once stood the great hall, the chapel, and the numerous buildings that housed the garrison.

Peter decided, as they drove back to Llanferon with the vicar, that he would come again, and this time by himself. Gwyn's half-bored interest was distracting, as was the vicar's booming voice, interesting though he was.

As the car turned the first corner in the winding old road, Peter turned his head, and looked back. Up on its staggering precipice, Carreg Cennen towered in dignified isolation, grim and fascinating, still dominating that lonely valley, as indeed it had done for the last nine hundred years, and as it probably would for many years to come.

Peter drew a sharp breath. Some curious instinct was tugging at his thoughts. He could not have explained it. He only knew that he must come back to Carreg Cennen.

The vicar broke in on his thoughts.

'You were impressed with Carreg Cennen, Peter?' he said, glancing for a second at Peter's absorbed expression.

Peter nodded. He was more than impressed, but it was not easy to find the right word.

'Natural, I suppose,' the vicar went on. 'With your family connection. Remote, of course, but still . . . You must come and see the de Blois tombs in the church.'

'Oh, are there some there, sir?'

'Several. And you can rub the brasses. That's a fascinating hobby.'

'Rubbing brasses?' Peter was puzzled; this was some-thing quite new to him.

They had reached the bottom of the drive leading to Mr Evans's house, and the vicar pulled up.

'Not heard of brass-rubbing?' he exclaimed. 'My dear boy, you've missed something.'

He was about to deliver one of his lectures, Peter felt, but he was anxious not to miss this particular one.

Anything that had any connection with the de Blois family or Carreg Cennen was interesting to him.

'In medieval days,' the vicar said, 'important people had a large sheet of brass put over their tomb. And a picture of the dead man was cut in the brass surface. It has lasted, you see, right down to this day, in perfect condition.'

'What about the rubbing, sir?' Peter asked.

'Ah, that's where the fun begins,' the vicar said with enthusiasm. 'The surface of the brass is rough, you see, after the picture has been cut. If you stretch a piece of special tracing-paper over it, and then rub with a stick of heel-ball, the engraving comes up in a perfect copy. And then you have a lovely specimen of a medieval portrait!'

'It sounds marvellous,' Peter said. 'But it must be pretty difficult to do, sir.'

'Good heavens, no!' the vicar said. 'I've done hundreds of them, and I can teach you the trick in a few minutes. Like to have a shot?'

Peter nodded. He certainly would like to try.

'Good! You'll learn something of history, too. With a good collection of brass rubbings, you can trace the whole history of medieval dress. Take armour, for instance.'

Peter was quite prepared to take armour. It was a subject that had always fascinated him.

'With brasses of armour,' the vicar exclaimed, 'you can follow the complete evolution of armour from the chain mail of the Normans, down to the elaborate plate armour of the late Plantagenets.'

He was in full flight now, and Peter and Gwyn listened dumbly to the stream of technical words; they were out of their depth in a few seconds, but that was beyond the vicar's notice. He spoke of camail, salades, bascinets, hauberks, vambraces, demi-brassarts, jambarts, and so on, until Peter's brain was numbed with the flow of curious names, half English, half Norman.

But the vicar moved gleefully on to maces, battle-axes, visors, misericordes, and tilting haumes, finishing up with a short conducted tour of the collection of armour in the Tower of London, and a few bitter remarks about the invention of firearms that had brought the great days of chivalry to an end.

The last war, they gathered from the vicar, was a drab and uninteresting affair. If General Montgomery had landed in Normandy clad in full plate armour, the vicar would have taken a great deal more interest in the campaign.

'All that quite clear?' demanded the vicar.

'Well, fairly, sir,' Peter said.

'I wonder. Well, see you tomorrow, then. Ten o'clock at the vicarage, and I'll take you both across to the church.'

Peter walked up the drive in silence, while Gwyn chattered about the castle. Peter was wondering ruefully if he would ever be able to learn anything about the subject of armour. It sounded horribly complicated, and it was a subject he would love to understand.

He little knew then how familiar he would become with all those elaborate technical expressions that the vicar had used. How could he have guessed?

3

BRASS-RUBBING

The vicar's study, when Peter saw it the next morning, was rather as he had expected to find it. It was filled with books; not only the walls, but most of the chairs, too, were piled up with books, in addition to the two small tables, and the large desk by the window.

'Ah, there you are,' the vicar said, 'I've got everything ready for you. Paper, and heel-ball . . . I think that's the lot.'

'Could we see some of your rubbings, sir?' Gwyn asked. He had become quite interested in this new hobby.

'Of course,' the vicar said.

He went over to a tall bookcase, and pulled open the long shallow drawers at the bottom. He returned with an armful of long white cylinders of paper, neatly tied with red tape.

Peter watched as the vicar untied the tape, and allowed the paper to unroll. Then he gasped.

For the vicar was holding a six-foot picture. Standing out in sharp relief against the white background was the life-size figure of a knight in armour, every detail etched in jet black, clear and beautifully distinct.

'Interesting, isn't it?' the vicar said with delight, pleased at the expression on the faces of the two boys. 'That's Sir John D'Aubernon. The oldest brass in existence. Yes, 1277, that's the date. Beautiful, isn't it?'

He showed them several more rubbings, and Peter began to learn something about armour even in that short time.

'Right, now let's go across to the church,' the vicar said.

Llanferon Church was quite small, but what it lacked in size, it more than gained in the beauty of its quiet dignity. Peter knew enough from his history lessons to recognize the typical Norman pillars, simple and massive, that ran up the centre of the nave, and he saw the curious zigzag ornamentation carved on the round arches of the windows.

'Recognize those arms, Peter?' the vicar asked him pointing to one of the windows.

Peter nodded. He had seen that coat of arms before, for his mother had it engraved on her silver. There was the familiar up-spread hand in an iron gauntlet . . . A gauntlet! There was always a gauntlet, he thought, connected with this particular business.

'Now, here's Roger de Blois,' the vicar said, tapping the worn grey stone of a large raised tomb.

Peter went across quickly, and bent over the large sheet of brass that was covering the top of the tomb.

'Roger's brass,' the vicar said. 'Fine specimen, too.'

Despite its great age, the brass still showed every detail with amazing clearness. Peter felt a trifle disappointed, though, for he had been expecting to see the figure of a knight in full armour. But Roger de Blois was very different from Peter's conception of a fourteenth-century knight.

The brass showed a figure of a man, with clasped hands, his feet resting on an animal with a curiously shaped head. Roger's head was covered with a dome-shaped helmet, and round the rest of his face was what seemed to Peter to resemble a balaclava helmet, though it was obviously made of steel.

Below that was an extremely odd garment, or so Peter thought, for coming down to Roger's waist was a long flowing robe, very much like a skirt. At the back, it fell to

the knees, but in front it was higher, and was parted to
show the end of Roger's mail shirt.

A huge sword hung from a belt round his waist, and his
left elbow was covered by a shield, emblazoned with the
sign of the gauntlet.

'He doesn't seem to have much armour,' Peter said in
disappointed tones.

'And he's wearing a skirt!' Gwyn said with disgust.

The vicar chuckled.

'Oh, not a skirt, Gwyn,' he said. 'A cyclas.' He went on
to explain the details of the brass, and for once, his
description was simple, and easy enough to follow.

'Armour started with mail,' he said. 'Heavy iron rings
sewn together, and fastened to a leather coat. Then they
began to add pieces of steel to the weakest spots, like the
knees and the elbows. At last, they had so many pieces of
steel, that the mail went altogether, and a knight wore a
complete suit of steel plate. Now Roger, here, was about
half-way; a mixture of plate and mail.'

The vicar's hand traced the thin lines round Roger's neck.

'Difficult to make a piece of steel plate fit there,' he said.
'Imagine yourself wearing an iron collar and scarf! You
wouldn't be able to move your head at all. So he wears a
mail coif, and it covers the vulnerable part of his neck and
throat. Then his arms are covered with plates. Strapped on
probably.'

'And on his legs,' Gwyn said.

'Knee pads, too,' said the vicar, 'and on his legs. You can
see the straps.'

'Like cricket pads,' Peter muttered, peering down at the
worn surface of the old brass.

'But what about the skirt?' Gwyn asked.

'The cyclas? It wasn't quite as silly as it looks. You
imagine yourself in that suit of armour on a hot sunny
day. You'd be grilled like a lobster!'

'I should jolly well think so,' muttered Gwyn emphatically.

'So Roger wore a white covering to keep off the sun,' the vicar said, warming up to his subject. 'And you could have your coat of arms embroidered on it, too. Just as well to let everyone know who you were, with all that stuff on, and a helmet covering your face. Otherwise, one of your friends might crack you over the head in the middle of a battle.'

He showed them the other tombs, including that of Henry de Blois, the last of his name to hold the castle of Carreg Cennen.

'And there's an extraordinarily interesting little brass over here,' he said, dragging them across the nave.

Peter looked up, and saw a small brass fixed to the wall. As his eyes fell on it, an odd feeling swept over him. The light seemed to grow dim and the grey stone of the wall in front of him swayed. Then his head cleared suddenly, and he bent forward to glance at the brass.

'Is it a boy?' he asked, seeing the small figure engraved on the brass sheet.

'Yes. A Peter de Blois, or so I believe,' the vicar said. 'I haven't been able to trace him at all in the family records, but he must have lived about the time of old Roger, over there,' and he waved his hand towards the tomb which they had been examining.

He started to walk away, followed by Gwyn. But Peter felt a curious reluctance to leave. He stared in silence at the brass of the unknown Peter de Blois, his head filled with a confused mass of jumbled thoughts and doubts. Then a shiver ran through him, he sighed, and turned away slowly.

A few seconds later he was being instructed in the art of brass-rubbing, and the vicar was stretching a sheet of paper over the brass of Roger de Blois for him. In the interest of rubbing, and watching the tiny details of the armour appear as if by magic under the slow pressure of the stick of heel-ball, Peter forgot his recent experience.

He was surprised at the speed with which he completed the rubbing. Gwyn was at the same kind of work on Henry de Blois, and they had both finished by lunch-time.

The vicar beamed at their efforts.

'Soon make expert rubbers out of you,' he said. 'Ah, you've done Henry de Blois, Gwyn. He was Roger's son: the last of the de Blois family. He was killed at Poitiers.'

'If I wanted to rub a brass in another church, would I be allowed to?' Peter asked.

'Of course, my dear boy,' the vicar said. 'Ask the vicar for permission first. In some churches they make a small charge towards the upkeep of the building, which is only fair enough, you know.'

'Do you charge people here, sir?' Peter asked.

The vicar chuckled, and gestured towards a small box fixed to one of the massive Norman pillars.

'I direct their attention to that,' he said.

As they went down the nave, Peter fumbled in his pocket. He was wondering if any of his week's pocket money was left, and with a sigh of relief pulled out a shilling, which he slipped into the collecting box. It seemed a small enough payment for a fascinating morning, he thought.

The vicar opened the door, and went out. Peter hesitated for a second, turned, and looked towards the chancel. A ray of watery sunshine was striking down through a window, and falling on some piece of metal on the wall beyond. It was the brass of the unknown Peter de Blois.

'Coming, Peter?' called out Gwyn from outside.

'Yes.' Peter shrugged his shoulders, and ran out into the sunshine.

4

The Gauntlet Again

The vicar's ancient car swayed dangerously, and jolted to a halt.

'Get a fine view from here,' he said, and jumped out.

It was two days later, and Gwyn and Peter had been driven over to see the abbey of Valle Crucis, a ruined monastery a few miles from Llanferon. Whoever had decided on the site, Peter thought, had chosen a lovely spot in the depths of the Welsh hills, and many miles from the nearest town. They were standing on the crest of a hill at that moment, and at their feet was a narrow valley, with a stream winding down the centre.

By the side of the stream was a huge sprawling mass of grey, half-ruined buildings, impressive and beautiful, even now, in decay.

'Yes, that's Valle Crucis,' the vicar said. ' "The Valley of the Cross." Lovely, isn't it? These old monks knew how to build.'

'Pretty lonely place,' Gwyn said.

'Ah, that was intentional,' the vicar said quickly. 'The Cistercians always buried themselves miles from anywhere.'

'The who, sir?' Peter asked.

'Cistercians,' the vicar repeated. 'There were several kinds of monks, you see, with different rules and ways of living. Benedictines, Carthusians, and so on.'

Another lecture coming, Peter thought. And he was quite right. For the next five minutes the by now familiar flow of long words streamed from the vicar's lips, strange

26

half-French, half-Latin words, such as refectories, scrip-
toriums, calefactories, cloisters, and dormitories.

The lecture came to an end with some extremely rude
comments on King Henry the Eighth, and the manner in
which that gentleman had dissolved the monasteries in the
sixteenth century.

'Now, let's go down, and have a closer look,' the vicar
said, and they rattled down the hill, negotiated the sharp
corner at the bottom, more by luck than good driving, and
drew up in front of the abbey.

Without the expert guidance of the vicar, neither of the
boys would have made much of the visit. For the abbey
was an enormous place, as Peter soon realized, and thanks
to the Ministry of Works, which had taken over the great
ruin, and preserved what the centuries with all their wear
and tear had left, there was a good deal to see.

They were led round at a brisk pace, with a running
commentary on the use of each part of the building, as the
vicar brought back to life the teeming activity of the vast
monastery, and the hundreds of people who had once
lived there in that lonely deserted valley.

Peter was beginning to learn a great deal about medieval
life. He was given the full use of Mr Evans's well-stocked
library, and by the end of the week he felt that he could
have found his way round a Cistercian abbey or a Norman
castle, and put on a suit of armour. He had rubbed all the
brasses in Llanferon Church, and was finishing the last
one, that of Henry de Blois, a few days later.

He was quite alone in the little church that afternoon.
But he was too absorbed in his work to feel lonely, though
it was dark in the nave. Outside, it was raining hard, and
Peter could hear the steady swish and gurgle of the rain in
the gutters.

He put the last finishing touches to the rubbing, and
stood back to inspect the result. He was improving, he

thought. Not even the vicar could have done better. But the light was fading, so he rolled up the stiff sheet of paper, and struggled into his mackintosh.

Half-way down the nave, on his way to the doors at the end, he hesitated, and then came to a dead stop. Some instinct was tugging his head round. It was not altogether a pleasant kind of instinct, either; there was a touch of eeriness about it. But Peter turned slowly, and looked up the long shadowy nave. He knew, without any doubt, that he must go back and look at that brass in the chancel.

With reluctant, dragging steps, he made his slow way to the choir stalls, crossed the narrow stone floor, and bent forward to peer at the blurred brass. Who *was* Peter de Blois, he wondered, with a feeling of horrified fascination. And why was there a brass to his memory in the church? It was unusual, the vicar had said, for a brass to be erected to a boy. Brasses were expensive luxuries, even in the Middle Ages.

The light was poor now, and the old church was full of faint whispering noises, the rain on the roof and the rustle of the bare trees outside in the wind.

Peter peered more closely. In that faint flickering light the figure in the brass had seemed to move. Peter caught his breath suddenly, and put out his hand.

'Is that you, Master Peter?' came a deep voice from behind.

Peter drew a long shuddering breath. He froze where he stood for a fraction of a second, and then whipped round.

'Gosh, you gave me a fright, Mr Davies,' he said, a wave of the most intense relief sweeping over him as he recognized the old verger.

'Ah, you were so intent like, Master Peter,' the old man said. 'The vicar said you would most likely be here, rubbing one of them brasses. Have you finished? I can lock up then.'

Peter thanked him, and five minutes later was trudging along in the driving rain. But it was not until he had finished tea, and was lounging in the depths of one of Mr Evans's big armchairs in front of a roaring fire, that he began to shake off the numb sensation of horror that had engulfed him in the church that afternoon.

But he did not sleep well that night. He dreamt of many confused incidents, of brasses, abbeys, and castles. One short fleeting dream was very vivid. He was standing on the hill above the castle of Carreg Cennen, and was staring down with amazement. For the grey walls had lightened, the gaps had been closed up, and from the tall gatehouse, he could see a huge banner waving lazily in the wind. Then the valley was blotted out with a damp, clinging mist, filled with shouts, the clang of arms, and the blaring of trumpets, high, shrill, and defiant.

With a jerk, Peter sat up in bed, and glared wildly round the room. It was very dark, and from outside came the steady whisper of the rain. The familiar sound soothed him, and he fell into a dreamless sleep.

Gwyn was late down to breakfast that morning, and when he did arrive, his face was drawn and white.

'Hullo, what's the matter with you?' Mr Evans asked quickly.

'Toothache, Uncle. Kept me awake most of the night.'

'Oh, I'm sorry; better see the dentist,' Mr Evans said.

Gwyn blenched.

'It's not as bad as all that, Uncle,' he said hurriedly.

'Quite sure? He's a good dentist. Won't give you a twinge.'

Gwyn considered the matter, and picked up his coffee cup. He took one sip, screwed up his face, and groaned.

'Ouch!' he muttered. 'Sore spot there.'

'You ought to have it out,' Mr Evans said grimly. 'I'll drive you in this morning before you change your mind.'

With some reluctance, Gwyn agreed, and both Peter and Mr Evans were relieved when the meal was over. Gwyn eating a hard-boiled egg in one corner of his mouth, to the accompaniment of frequent groans, was not a cheerful table companion.

'Want to come, Peter?' Mr Evans asked, as he brought the car round to the front of the house.

Peter shook his head. He had been doing some quick thinking. The rain had cleared off, and he had already planned out his morning.

'If you don't mind, Mr Evans,' he said. 'There's not much point, is there?'

He watched the car disappear. Gwyn was sitting by his uncle, and he waved dolefully to Peter. By his expression he might have been going to hospital for a major operation, and his other hand was holding on to his jaw as if he were expecting it to fall off at any moment.

Peter grinned, and went inside. He waited for about ten minutes, and then went out again. He walked briskly, and with the air of a person who had braced himself for an expedition that might be both exciting and dangerous.

The castle was quite deserted, for it was too early in the day for visitors, and there were never many at that time of the year. Peter spent a peaceful hour exploring, his vivid imagination re-filling the old ruin with its inhabitants, and restoring the fallen stones and towers. He clambered up a winding half-ruined stair by the gatehouse, and found himself in a small round room. The roof had disappeared long ago, and one side of the wall had crumbled away, leaving the room open to the elements above and below.

But there was enough there for Peter to reconstruct the original appearance of the room. He could see the fireplace, and the holes in the thick walls where beams of wood had once held up the stone roof. In one corner was a ruined doorway. But it led nowhere now. Peter put his head through, and then recoiled. For there was nothing outside: just a sheer drop to the courtyard below.

Below there had once stood the hall, he knew, from what the vicar had said, and the living-rooms of the lord of the castle. Peter leant against the stone window, and looked across the valley, to the brown hills beyond. He thought idly that Peter de Blois might have once stood there and stared out from this window at the same view. Those hills could not have altered much in the last five hundred years or so.

A hoarse blare of a horn jolted Peter back to the twentieth century. A large yellow bus had just pulled up on the road below, and a string of people were making their way up to the castle.

Peter groaned. 'Trippers!' he muttered with disgust. They would be swarming all over the place in a minute, taking photographs, and making stupid remarks about the romantic grey walls.

With a final snort, Peter scrambled down the stairs, ducked behind a pile of stones, and watched the visitors stream past into the castle. He felt antagonistic towards the new arrivals. This was his castle, he thought, as he ran down the slope, and burst out on to the road.

But he was reluctant to leave just yet. He wandered up the road, and stopped by a gap in the hedge. The sun was pleasantly warm now, and there was a convenient stone ledge just below, from where he could get a good view of the castle. He dropped down into the ditch, and sat himself on the wide stone. Immediately below him was the ugly yellow splash of the bus. He lifted his head to the castle; he could see heads on the walls now, as the trippers wandered around.

Might as well wait until they went, he decided, after a glance at his wrist watch. It was just after eleven. Far too early to expect Mr Evans and Gwyn back from the dentist.

He wriggled himself into a more comfortable position in the hedge, and leant his head against the stone. It was warm there, out of the wind, and in the sun. He yawned, and stretched himself lazily. Curious, but he felt sleepy. Peter's head dropped, jerked up again, but once more his eyes began to droop.

Peter never knew quite how long he did sleep. But he supposed that he must have slept—perhaps for an hour, or even longer. He was to puzzle over that for many years afterwards. But his last conscious recollection was the sound of an aeroplane engine as the plane flew overhead, and droned away into the distance.

He awoke with a start. He felt hot, and half dazed, as if he had slept heavily. His head was buzzing, and one arm was hanging down, aching and cramped. He was holding something. He lifted his hand, and gasped, his eyes round with incredulous surprise.

For he was holding a heavy iron gauntlet.

5

ROGER DE BLOIS

Peter stared down at the gauntlet. There was no doubt in his mind; it was the gauntlet which he had found up on Carn Eglwys. But he was not worrying about that; he was trying to decide whether he was frightened or pleased. When he had started out that morning, it was with the faint hope that somehow he might find the gauntlet, and now that he had . . .

He sighed and looked blankly through the hedge. He stiffened. The yellow bus had gone. And what was that building at the foot of the slope leading up to the castle? He had not noticed it before. And the sun. It was beating down on him with the heat of midsummer.

But he had no time to think over these changes. For behind, on the road, he heard a sound that made him wheel round. It was the blast of a trumpet, and the thud of hooves. They came closer, a horse galloping at full speed, and in the background, Peter could distinguish a curious jangling sound. Some farmer riding into Llanferon, he thought, and stepped out into the road.

The horse shot into view over the crest of the hill, and was pulled up with a jerk, its forefeet leaving the ground, as its rider reined him in . . . His rider! Peter gasped, his mouth opening with silent and speechless surprise. For sitting in the high saddle, one hand on his hip, was a man in full armour.

Peter rubbed his eyes, but the man was still there. Must be a film, Peter thought. The cameramen will arrive in a minute. And whoever was in charge of the film knew what

33

he was doing, Peter decided, examining the man with all the expert knowledge which he had acquired from his reading in the last week.

A huge dome-shaped helmet covered the man's head, coming down to his shoulders, and fitted with an iron visor, the sharp point jutting out like the peak of a cricket cap. His shoulders and arms were covered with a fine mesh of mail armour, the steel rings highly polished, and glittering in the sunlight. Long metal plates were strapped around his arms and legs, and his general appearance and equipment were startlingly similar to that of the fourteenth-century brass of Roger de Blois in Llanferon Church. He was even wearing a cyclas, which fell in long graceful folds over his knees. His face was turned away from Peter, and it was impossible to see the design on the front of the cyclas, or on the face of the big shield that hung from his left arm.

The horse shifted uneasily, and turned. Peter could see the badge now, both on the cyclas and the shield. It was a familiar and astonishing coat of arms, and there was no mistaking it in that hard clear sunlight.

It was the sign of the Gauntlet.

The horseman looked down the road as his horse shifted, saw Peter, and clapped his spurs to his horse's side. With a jingle of armour, he pulled up beside the dazed figure of Peter.

'Ah, Peter,' he said, 'you have found it.' He held out a bare hand.

Peter instinctively obeyed the gesture, and held out the gauntlet which he was holding.

'Good boy,' the man said. He leant down, and clapped Peter on the shoulder. 'You shall have a silver penny for your pains. Now, where in the fiend's name is Robert?'

He stood up in his stirrups, and looked back along the road. If it could be called a road, Peter thought. What on earth had happened to the black tarred surface? There was nothing to be seen but a rutted and stony track that would have ruined the springs of any modern car in five minutes.

His eyes had dropped to the road, and with the same glance he saw his feet. He gasped again; the first of many such exclamations from him that day. His feet! Gone were his brown shoes. Instead he was wearing rough leather sandals, with long sharp points. And his grey flannel shorts? All he could see, as he squinted down at his legs, were tight green stockings, reaching up to his knees. In a daze, he held out his hands. His blazer had gone too. Now, he was wearing a long-sleeved kind of sweater, of the same colour as the stockings, and over that a white coat, with wide sleeves finishing short at the elbows, and the skirt coming down to his knees.

There was some badge embroidered on the breast of his coat. Peter peered down. But even looking at it upside down, there was no difficulty in seeing the design. It was that of the silver Gauntlet.

With a stifled gasp, Peter put his hands up instinctively to his head. But even that simple gesture gave him a fresh shock. For his hands touched long hair falling down to his shoulders.

'Ah, Robert at last!' the horseman said, breaking in on poor Peter's whirling thoughts.

He looked up sharply. He felt prepared to see anything now. His brain was so numbed that he felt incapable of finding any explanation for the incredible events around him. It was with no particular surprise that he saw two horses appear on the road. A man, wearing a rough leather jerkin, and a steel helmet, was riding the first horse, and he was leading a pony with his free hand.

'Peter is here,' the first horseman said curtly, as the new arrival reined up beside them.

The second man raised his hand in a rough salute, and grinned at Peter. He had a red weather-beaten face, craggy and seamed, with a vivid red scar down the right cheek.

'I had made a cast up the mountain, Lord Roger,' he said.

Peter stiffened. Lord Roger!

'Quick, Peter, into the saddle,' the first man said sharply. 'We are late. Your lady mother will be worried enough as it is, God knows.'

Peter was pushed up into the saddle of the pony. He took the reins, and instinctively pressed his knees into the pony's side as it followed the two other horses, which had already started off down the track. They turned the corner at the bottom of the hill, and started the climb up to the castle. Over their heads was the menacing bulk of the great walls and towers, and Peter gazed up. Then he stood up in his stirrups, a strangled exclamation of astonishment coming from his lips. His pony, startled by the sudden tug on the reins, pulled up abruptly.

There was Carreg Cennen Castle clearly enough. But it had changed out of all semblance from the majestic ruin that he had often admired. The grey walls had lightened, the broken gaps had disappeared, the massive towers stood complete, their sides bare and clean of ivy. Over the great gatehouse waved a huge red banner, flapping lazily in the faint breeze.

It was the picture he had seen in his dream, Peter thought. But it was all extraordinarily clear now. He could even see the sun flashing on the helmets of the sentries on the walls, and as he plucked at his reins to catch up the two riders in front, he could hear the high clear call of a trumpet from the gatehouse, shrill and insistent, sending the blood coursing through his veins with a sudden thrill of excitement.

The leading rider was waving to him. Instinctively, Peter waved back, and trotted up the slope. Lucky I can ride, he was thinking. But there was no thought of not joining the other two men. Peter was like a man who has fallen into a fast-flowing current, his brain numbed by the shock of the accident, and content to float, carried along to . . . what? Peter's brain was incapable of giving him an answer.

They reached the gatehouse. Even in a ruined condition it had been impressive. But now, with its full height restored, it was stupendous, towering up above Peter's head, grim and forbidding in its stark clear outlines.

They were inside the courtyard now, after clattering over a wooden drawbridge. Peter threw a dazed glance around the crowded busy courtyard, filled with swarms of people. But he had no time to see more. A hand nudged his knee. It was Robert, who had already dismounted.

Peter threw one leg over, and slid to the ground. Someone led away the pony. Peter caught a brief glimpse of a leather coat, and the sign of the Gauntlet, and then he was blindly following the broad back of Robert, who was half-way through the nearest doorway.

He was climbing a steep spiral staircase. With an amused smile at the absurdity of the situation, he recognized it for the staircase up which he had climbed that morning. The thought had barely crossed his dazed mind when Robert threw open the door at the top of the stairs, bowed, and stood aside for Peter to pass.

There was no doubt about the room. It was the one in which he had stood; there was the window, looking across the valley to Llanferon and the mountains beyond. There was no glass, but a small wooden shutter was hinged back against the wall. No glass in the fourteenth century, Peter remembered, except for the churches with their beautiful stained-glass windows.

In the fourteenth century! Peter shivered, and looked round wildly for some familiar object, a telephone, a book, a wireless set, anything that would assure him that he was not in the middle of some frightful nightmare. But all that he saw was the bare circular room with its rough stone walls, and the rough good-humoured face of Robert, who was looking at him in surprise.

'Shall I bring your bath, my lord?' he asked. 'You are tired perhaps, after the ride.'

'Er . . . yes, I am,' muttered Peter.

The door clanged behind Robert, and Peter staggered against the wall, his hands up to his face. A wave of panic swept over him, and he groaned. Perhaps if I pinch myself, he thought a trifle desperately, I shall wake up, and find myself back in bed in Mr Evans's house. So he pinched himself viciously in the arm, winced, and opened his eyes. He looked down, and there were the long toes of his shoes, and the green of his stockings. He stared round the room, praying that by some miracle the walls might dissolve, and the wooden ceiling disappear. Try the window, his terrified brain said, and he pushed his head outside.

There were the mountains; they had not changed, at any rate; and with a thrill of sudden hope, Peter saw the squat grey tower of Llanferon church. It *must* be a dream, he repeated to himself, and glanced to the right, where he knew he could see the roof of Mr Evans's house, Llysmeddyg.

But there was nothing there. Just the bare slopes of the hill, a few scattered trees, a dash of darker foliage, but no house, no drive, no barns or stables. Nothing!

The door opened, and Robert staggered in with a great tub of hot water. He dropped it, and stared at Peter with a grunt, and a grin. It was a friendly and reassuring grin to

Peter, clutching frantically for anything reassuring in this nightmare world into which he had been plunged so suddenly. Though Robert could not have been described as a particularly prepossessing sight, with his brown face, vivid red scar and his toothless grin.

He poured the water into a wooden tub by the window, and then opened a great chest standing against the wall.

'I will lay out your clothes, my lord,' he said.

Peter nodded. I must pull myself together, he thought miserably. Better have a bath, I suppose. Mustn't do anything to give the game away. What sort of game, he thought, as he started to struggle with the unfamiliar clothes. It doesn't matter what I do or say. Nobody would believe me if I did tell them the truth. They'd just think I was mad.

He pulled off the surcoat, and then found that he was wearing a rough vest underneath that. The long green stockings were awkward, but fortunately Robert was used to that, for he gave Peter a hand.

As he dipped his bare foot gingerly in the hot water, a cold draught eddied through the window. He shivered. Castles might look very beautiful and impressive, he thought, but they were certainly not palaces of luxury. Still, the hot water was pleasant enough, and he relaxed gratefully. It was a relief to know that some people did wash in the Middle Ages. The history books were full of the filth and dirt of those days, but he had read somewhere that the knights and nobles were fond of hot baths.

That bath did Peter good; it soothed him. And the business of dressing afterwards was fascinating enough to drive away the frightening thoughts that were chasing across his mind.

It was just as well that he had a servant to help him, Peter reflected, otherwise he would not have known where to start. Robert pulled a silken under-vest over his head first, and then paused.

'The scarlet hose, my lord?' he asked.

Peter nodded. The colour of the long stockings was a trifle startling after the drab colours worn by the men in the twentieth century, but he liked dressing up as much as any normal boy. The hose were more like a pair of tight trousers, as they came up as far as his waist, and were held in place by strings. Robert knelt down and put a pair of long leather slippers on Peter's feet. These shoes were soft and extremely comfortable, though the pointed toes were inclined to flap as he walked.

'The best cote-hardie?' Robert asked. 'The Lady Marian has guests.'

Peter nodded. He had no idea what Robert was talking about, and the reference to Lady Marian had startled him. Who on earth was she? he wondered dismally. His mother? The Lord Roger was presumably his father. This was all getting incredibly complicated.

Robert held out a coat, the cote-hardie, Peter assumed. It was a gorgeous looking garment; a tightly fitting coat that came down as far as his waist, with buttons fastening in front. The sign of the silver Gauntlet was embroidered on the breast, and the sleeves and shoulders were resplendent with gold and silver decorations.

A thin leather belt was fastened round him, and Peter glanced curiously at the small dagger on the left-hand side, and the purse on the right. He wondered what was inside that; he must have a look when he was by himself. Then Robert draped a garment round him that completely baffled Peter. It was in the form of a combined hood and cape, of scarlet, and the point of the hood was extended into a long thin pipe that trailed down his back. Robert threw the hood over his head, and arranged it carefully on his shoulders. He noticed the puzzled expression on Peter's face and smiled.

''Tis indeed a strange fashion, the liripipe, my lord,' he said. 'But there is no end to these new-fangled ideas.'

Liripipe, thought Peter. He had come across the name in Mr Evans's books, but had vaguely assumed that it was some kind of musical instrument.

'There, my lord,' Robert said, as he picked up a rough comb, and ran it through Peter's long hair, leaving him with a fringe over the forehead, and sweeping the rest back. Just like a girl, Peter thought with disgust. I must look an awful sight.

He glanced round instinctively for a mirror, and Robert, who must have read his thoughts, handed him a highly-polished piece of steel. It was a poor mirror by modern standards, and Peter could do no more than examine himself in sections. But he was pleasantly struck with his appearance. The dress of the Middle Ages might be strange to his twentieth-century mind, but it was certainly magnificent.

Robert chuckled behind his back.

'Have no fear, my lord,' he said. 'You are a real de Blois.'

Well, I've learnt my name, Peter thought. He was wondering what he was supposed to do next, and he looked towards Robert, who as usual solved the problem for him. The man had opened another door in a corner of the room, and was standing there for Peter to move past him.

Peter took a step forward, and paused. He had looked through that door earlier in the day. But there had been nothing on the other side then. Nothing but a sheer drop to the courtyard below. Well, if he was a de Blois, he had better behave like one, and he went bravely forward. Ahead of him stretched a long narrow passage, with stone floors, and bare stone walls. The right-hand side was pierced with thin slits, through which shone the last rays of the evening sun.

As he walked hesitantly forward, glancing curiously through the arrow slits, Peter's hands fumbled instinctively by his side, and with a grin he realized that he was trying to find his pockets. Well, he had none now.

At the end of the passage was another door, half open, and as Peter reached it, he heard the sound of laughing voices from the other side. He stopped abruptly, another wave of panic rushing down upon him.

Robert, who had followed him down the passage, slipped past, and opened the door. He did not think it odd that Peter should have stopped by the door. Opening doors was clearly beneath the dignity of a de Blois when his servant was there to do the work.

Peter found himself just inside the room, and the door clanged behind him. With the disappearance of Robert, he felt that the one familiar and reassuring thing he had yet found in this strange world had deserted him. He felt lonely, scared, and bewildered.

The room in which he found himself was long and narrow. On the left was a huge fireplace, and logs were smouldering there fitfully. Above the fire, which smoked badly, the chimney soared up to the wooden rafters of the ceiling in the shape of a great hood. The walls of the room were covered with coloured tapestries, and immediately in front of Peter was a tall window, but without any glass. The shutters were folded back, and below them was a deep window seat.

Peter took in these details in one rapid and nervous glance and then his attention was caught by the people who were standing or sitting by the fireplace. He had a vague impression of bright clothes, brilliant colours, and two men, a woman, and two boys. But their faces swam in front of his eyes in a blurred vision.

Then the woman turned, and saw him standing by the door.

'Ah, Peter, my son,' she said. 'We have been waiting for you.'

She held up her hand, and beckoned him forward.

Peter gulped, and took a few uncertain steps forward towards the group.

6

A Medieval Dinner

As Peter pulled himself together with a great effort and stepped forward, the faces of the people in front of him suddenly seemed to jump into focus, as if he had been turning the knobs of a pair of binoculars on some distant object.

The Lady Marian was a tall stately woman with fair hair which was even more elaborately dressed than that of any modern lady. She wore a thin band of gold around her head, inset with jewels that caught the sunlight falling through the window behind her. Her skirt, long and flowing, was beautifully brocaded with silver threads, a lovely pattern that shimmered with every movement. Over the skirt, but cut to show the full lines, was another kind of overskirt, long and covered with white fur. The general effect was a little awe-inspiring to Peter, but one glance at her face reassured him. It was a cheerful, kindly face, and she was smiling at him with obvious affection.

She touched his arm, and guided him towards a high wooden chair facing the fire. The occupant was a man in white robes, and tonsured head. He turned to look at Peter.

For a second, the room swam in front of Peter, and he stifled a quick gasp. For the man in the chair, in spite of his abbot's robes, was the Vicar of Llanferon.

So it was a joke after all, Peter thought, and glanced swiftly to his right where a boy was standing. He had guessed right. For the boy was Gwyn. Peter smiled, and was about to speak, when a chilly spasm of doubt stopped

44

him in the nick of time. For the man in the chair and the boy were regarding him with the polite interest of total strangers. And as for the vicar, he might be dressed up, but all his white hair had totally disappeared, except for the thin circular line of the tonsure running round the top of his head.

'He is bemused, my Lord Abbot,' the Lady Marian said, touching Peter again.

The abbot chuckled, and held out his hand. The light flashed on a very heavy gold ring.

'Kneel, my son,' he said.

Peter was indeed bemused. He dropped obediently to one knee, and felt the abbot's hand touch his head, while the old man muttered a swift patter of words in Latin.

The abbot smiled at him as he stood up again, and turned to Roger de Blois.

'A fine boy, my Lord,' he said.

'He will pass,' Lord Roger said. But he shot Peter a quick glance of affection and pride.

'And he has quite recovered?' the abbot said, turning to the Lady Marian.

'Completely,' the Lady Marian said. 'It was a long illness, my Lord Abbot. But this doctor of my brother's has some curious ideas. He said that the mountain air in the winter was bad for the boy. Send him to the South, he told me. So Peter has spent the past four years with my brother in his castle in Surrey. He is almost a stranger to us. And I expect he will find much here that is strange to him.'

Peter tried to hide a quick smile. This was a stroke of luck, he thought, though he did wonder what illness it was from which he had been suffering. Still, it had been a convenient disease, whatever it was.

He would have liked to shrink aside and take in all the details of this incredible scene. But he was given no chance, for his mother, or so already he was thinking of her, pushed him forward once more.

'This is the Lord Glyndwr Llewellyn,' she said. 'You remember, Peter, that he was coming to live here as a page.'

'Er . . . yes,' Peter mumbled. He bobbed his head to Gwyn, who bowed back in silence, and with an air of indifferent scorn.

'A noble family, the Llewellyns,' remarked the abbot. 'You do well, my Lord Roger, to have him at the castle.'

'He will be company for Peter,' Roger said. 'And it is the king's wish that we live on good terms with the Welsh chieftains.'

They chatted idly, and Peter was at last able to step aside and watch them. The Lord Roger was a magnificent figure, with his great height and superb clothes. He wore scarlet hose and yellow cote-hardie, with a great silver Gauntlet embroidered on the breast. His face was dark, with a determined chin, and restless alert grey eyes. But though there was about him an air of supreme self-confidence, natural to a man whose word was law, and probably a matter of life or death to those who lived in the castle, his expression was pleasant, and his laugh infectious.

Peter suddenly noticed another boy by the window. He was about five years old, Peter thought, and was dressed in the usual hose, a gaily coloured cote-hardie, a yellow hood and liripipe.

He caught Peter's glance, and grinned.

'Will you come riding with me tomorrow, Peter?' he asked.

'Of course,' Peter said hastily, wondering who this could be, though his face seemed strangely familiar.

But the Lady Marian came to his rescue. 'That is kind of you, Peter,' she said, 'but it is time for you to go to bed, Henry.'

As the boy drifted reluctantly out of the room, Peter racked his brains. Henry? Of course, he suddenly remembered what the vicar had told him about the de Blois family history: Henry, the son of Roger, was the last of the male line of the family at Carreg Cennen, for he was killed at Poitiers.

Peter shivered suddenly and uncontrollably, despite the heat of the room. It was uncanny to think that he knew the future history of these people. It was only a few days ago that he had rubbed the brass on Roger's tomb. And the abbot? He must be from Valle Crucis. If so, Peter had seen the ruins of that vast abbey, and the corner of the abbey church where, it was believed, the abbots had been buried.

They were all ghosts, these people; they had died hundreds of years ago. And what about Peter de Blois? If Henry was the last of the line, what had happened to Peter? Why was that brass erected in Llanferon church?

But the Lady Marian had noticed his shiver, and she spoke quickly.

'You are chilled, Peter?' she said. 'Warm yourself by the fire.'

Peter did as he was told, and the pleasant warmth of the log fire calmed him down, whilst the conversation went on quietly around him. He was distracted a few minutes later by the blare of a trumpet from the depths of the castle.

'Supper,' announced Roger de Blois with satisfaction. 'I am starving. You are a good trencherman, my Lord Abbot, I remember?'

'I am indeed,' the abbot said emphatically, jumping to his feet. There was an expectant look on his red face as he swept out of the room, a dignified figure in his flowing white robes, which Peter remembered was the colour worn by the Cistercian monks.

They all went down a narrow staircase, through a door at the bottom, and emerged into the great hall of Carreg Cennen Castle. Peter gasped, and halted for a moment, for it was certainly a most incredible sight. He had an impression of a vast space, vivid blinding colour, a close-packed mass of faces, and a tremendous amount of noise. The atmosphere was thick and stuffy, filled with the scent of wood smoke.

The hall was a single-storied building with a high wooden roof. Peter, however, did not take much notice of the architecture, for he was far too interested in the people there. The long tables down the centre of the hall were surrounded by swarms of them, the men in violently-hued cote-hardies and hose, long dangling liripipes, and women with dresses of all the colours in the rainbow. There was little of the delicate shades of modern times; here there were no half measures. If a man had a scarlet tunic, it really was scarlet, bright and harsh in its simple primitive colour.

Peter was still trying to take in this extraordinary scene, when he found himself sitting on a hard backless stool on the dais at the top end of the hall. As he sat down there came the blare of trumpets from the other end, and a small procession advanced towards the dais. This was presumably the first course, but as the servers approached, Peter saw that they were carrying large basins and napkins.

The Lady Marian nudged Peter.

'It is time that you learnt the duties of a page, Peter,' she said. 'Take a ewer of water to the Lord Roger, and you, Glyndwr, one to the Lord Abbot. And see that you serve them on bended knee.'

Peter scrambled to his feet, took a firm grip on a basin of heavy silver which one of the servants held out to him, and went down clumsily on his knee behind Lord Roger's chair.

Lord Roger smiled at him, and then dipped the tips of his fingers in the water, before drying them on the napkin. It was not a particularly thorough wash, Peter thought, as he went back to his stool.

The servants withdrew, and emerged again from the kitchens at the lower end of the hall, the trumpets once more sounding as they marched up the space between the tables.

Peter was pushed to his feet once more by the Lady Marian, and helped Lord Roger to soup. It was good soup, too, he thought, as he tasted it. But he was startled by the noise around him. He had been taught to eat his soup with the minimum of noise; these people seemed to be making as much row as possible, as they gobbled and slushed their way through the soup. The abbot reminded Peter of a thirsty horse, and the old man was smacking his lips appreciatively as each mouthful went down with a gurgle.

The next course was fish, several varieties of them. As Peter took his place behind Lord Roger, his new parent leant back and inspected the dishes.

'Now, my Lord Abbot,' he said encouragingly, 'what will you? Trout, tench, or eel?'

The abbot needed no encouragement. He ran his eyes over the heaped-up dishes.

'Indeed, indeed, my lord,' he said doubtfully, as if he would have preferred the whole lot. 'Tench, I think. Yes, tench.'

A huge plateful of fish was put on the silver plate in front of him, and he beamed at the sight, rubbing his hands with undisguised glee. Peter grinned, and went back to where Robert was dishing out fish on his plate. It looked good, too, Peter thought, as he sat down, and put out his hands for the fish knife and fork.

There was a knife by the side of his plate, a beautifully carved one of silver; but where was the fork? With a feeling of dismay, Peter remembered that forks had not been invented in the fourteenth century. He glanced hurriedly to his left, to see what Lady Marian and the others were doing. It was quite simple, he saw. The abbot, Lord Roger, and Lady Marian were cutting up the fish, and the large helpings were going into their mouths in fingerloads, to the accompaniment of loud noises of appreciation.

Peter turned back, and eyed his fish with horror. But the Lady Marian came to his help, or so she thought. For she proceeded to give him a lesson in medieval table manners.

'Now, remember, my son,' she said. 'Do not dip your fish in the salt, and never more than two fingers and a thumb on the fish or meat. And on no account must you wipe your fingers on the table cloth. And mark you the same, Glyndwr.'

Peter nodded dumbly, and started to tackle the fish. But it was a messy business. The chief difficulty was to fill his mouth without allowing portions of hot moist fish to drop back with a watery squelch on to the plate again. He watched the others. They were like pigs at a trough, he thought with disgust.

A loud belch from Lord Roger announced that he had finished his fish course, and he cleared what was left on his plate by the extremely simple device of hurling the dregs on to the floor. Two dogs rushed up, and made a dash for the food, snapping and snarling in the straw rushes on the floor.

'Now, mark you, Peter,' Lady Marian said, who had watched the incident with approval, 'take heed from your father. Never fondle the dogs in the middle of the meal. If you wish to feed them, throw the meat to them.'

Peter mumbled something, his eyes popping with amazement. He wiped his filthy fingers on a napkin, and went behind Lord Roger's chair for the next course. A bewildering variety of dishes arrived, and the two men examined them with delighted interest.

'Geese, my lord?' Roger asked. 'Or perhaps venison, or kid?'

The abbot finally decided on lamb, but not before he had run an expert and loving eye over the other dishes. Probably going to have a shot at them too, Peter thought, for by this time he had gained a healthy respect for the old gentleman's appetite. Cabbages and onions completed the enormous helpings, but there was surely something missing, Peter thought, and with an effort he realized that there were no potatoes. When were potatoes invented, he wondered. Something to do with Sir Walter Raleigh; that must be in . . . he did a rough sum in his head; about two hundred years' time. A long time to wait for a potato.

'Peter, wine for the abbot,' Lord Roger said sharply.

Peter looked round helplessly. But the faithful Robert was standing behind, and he thrust a silver goblet into Peter's hands. The abbot watched his tankard being filled, tasted the wine, and then smacked his lips loudly. He hiccuped politely to show his appreciation, and turned to Lord Roger.

'Excellent, my lord,' he said. 'I have no better butt of malmsey in the abbey cellars.'

Peter slipped back to his place, and started to eat the piece of goose which Robert had put on his plate. At least, he carved a piece of the breast, and then paused doubtfully. How on earth could he deal with meat and vegetables without a fork? After some hesitation, he piled some cabbage on a portion of meat, and gingerly lifted the helping into his mouth with his fingers. The Lady Marian beamed her approval at his good table manners.

On his right, Glyndwr was eating in silence. He had not said a single word to Peter since the meal had started. Probably shy, Peter thought, as he's just arrived at the castle. Then he chuckled. Talk about just arriving. What about himself?

As he waded slowly and messily through the goose, Peter gazed around the table. Immediately in front of him was a huge silver ornament, in the shape of a ship. It was filled with spices, to which the others were helping themselves liberally, much to Peter's surprise, for he found the food was quite heavily spiced already. But as he remembered from his reading, the people of medieval days loved to drown the taste of their food with spices.

Among the ornaments which he noticed was the salt-cellar. There were small ones for Peter and Glyndwr, whilst the abbot and Lord Roger shared the great cellar in the centre of the table. Peter noticed that his little 'nef' or ship, had a space for his napkin and spoon.

By this time he had finished the breast of the goose, and had come to the leg. It seemed a pity to leave such a nice piece of meat, and he was still hungry. He tried to cut it into small portions, but without a fork it was far from simple.

How was the Lady Marian dealing with the problem? Peter glanced to his left; his mouth opened, and then shut with horrified surprise. For that stately lady was holding the leg of goose daintily between her fingers, and was tearing huge pieces away with her strong teeth. She finished, inspected the leg to see if there was any more meat, shook her head, and hurled the bone to the nearest dog. Then she wiped away the gravy which was trickling down her chin, and started on another piece.

Peter blinked, and turned away. Down the long tables in the centre of the hall, the servants of the castle were

She . . . hurled the bone to the nearest dog

(see page 52)

enjoying their meal. Great hunks of beef were being
served, and as Peter watched them, he saw men and
women gnawing away with their teeth as if they were
animals who had not eaten for several days.

'Well, here goes,' he thought, and lifted the leg of goose
to his mouth. There was nothing wrong with the taste, and
once he had learnt not to allow the gravy to trickle down
on to his cote-hardie, he enjoyed his meal. But his fingers
were a sight when he had finished.

The abbot and Lord Roger had passed on to the
venison, washing down the mouthfuls with large draughts
of wine. Peter wondered how many meals in the day these
people had, for this seemed a queer hour for dinner. He
glanced down instinctively at his left wrist. But there was
no familiar wrist watch there now.

The abbot leant back, and smiled benevolently at his
host. He had made a good meal, but there was more to
come. Peter heard the trumpets, and another procession
advanced towards the dais. At that moment the Lady
Marian leant forward reprovingly to Glyndwr.

'Glyndwr,' she said sharply. 'You must not blow your
nose with the same hand as that with which you have been
eating.'

Glyndwr dropped his hand with a guilty expression.
There was a large smudge of gravy on his nose.

'The other hand,' the Lady Marian said. 'And you must
turn away from the table. Like this.'

She put one shapely hand to her nose, seized it between
finger and thumb, turned her head away from the table,
and blew violently.

'Mark that, Glyndwr,' she said, 'and you, too, Peter.'

Peter nodded speechlessly. He wondered wildly what
she would do next. Probably spit on the floor. He was
quite right.

'And mark, too,' she continued. 'Never spit on the table. Watch the Lord Roger,' and she gestured to her left, where the Lord Roger was suiting the action to the word, an example which the Lady Marian followed as she spat out a piece of gristle on to the floor.

But she had not finished. She peered suspiciously into Peter's tankard.

'Peter!' she exclaimed in horror. 'I have told you before, never to leave the dregs in the cup. Throw them on to the floor.'

Peter picked up the heavy tankard, and obediently emptied the dregs of the wine on to the sodden rushes at his feet.

The Lady Marian nodded with approval, and turned her attention to the next course. This consisted of pastries and tarts, made in all kinds of fantastic shapes. The main dish was in the form of a rough model of a church, presumably in honour of the abbot, who clapped his hands with delight.

'A most noble subtlety,' he said, 'you do me great honour, my lord,' and he plunged his spoon into the heart of the pie.

It was an apple-pie, Peter discovered, as he tackled the huge helping that Robert gave him. His plate, he noticed, was always the same one. After each course, it was whipped away, and wiped by one of the servants.

The long meal came to an end at last, and the light in the hall was fading. Servants went round, lighting long wax candles which stood in silver holders on the high table. This, as Peter learnt afterwards, was not always done, for candles were expensive items in those days. The rest of the hall was lighted with torches placed in holders on the walls. They did not give a very effective light, and they spluttered furiously, and gave off a good deal of thick acrid smoke.

But despite the close atmosphere, the smoke and the smells of hot spiced food and the stuffiness of the air, the great hall presented an astonishing sight to Peter, looking at it with his twentieth-century eyes.

Up on the dais at the high table, the soft lights of the candles flashed on the jewels and barbaric ornaments, whilst the magnificent clothes with their vivid harsh shades were in startling contrast to the patches of gloom. For most of the hall was in comparative darkness now. The torches did no more than throw a patchy light; the huge fire, piled high with logs, cast a hard angry glare from the wall on the left. Soaring up above was the lofty roof, lost to sight now in the gathering darkness, a vast mass of shadowy space. It was a bewildering, unbelievable pageant of bright colours, wild beauty, and dark shadows.

Meanwhile, the tables had been cleared, and Lord Roger was suggesting an entertainment for his guest. Peter heard him mention a Welsh harpist, and the man appeared presently, to take up a place just below the dais. He was an uncouth-looking fellow, with untidy black hair, and wearing shabby clothes. As he ran his fingers across the strings of his harp, Peter noticed Glyndwr bend forward, his face alight with the first sign of animation he had shown that night.

Peter was disappointed with the song. Perhaps it was because he was more used to modern music, but he found the tune flat and monotonous, though there was a note of savage fury in the second song that the man sang. Peter found it curiously disturbing, and by his side he could hear Glyndwr breathing heavily, and stirring restlessly in his seat.

Lord Roger fumbled in the purse hanging from his belt, and hurled a coin to the harpist with the same casual air with which he had thrown food to the dogs. Peter's head began to droop. His eyes were stinging with the smoke, and his head felt numbed and tired. The noise of applause for the harpist, the thundering din of tankards being thumped on the wooden tables echoed like thunder in his ears.

It was with tremendous relief that he heard the Lady Marian suggest that it was time for him and Glyndwr to go to bed. Peter stumbled to his feet, bobbed his head to the others, and followed Robert up the staircase to his room. Behind him he could hear the roar of voices from the hall.

Peter's small circular room seemed a haven of peace after the noise and confusion of the hall. A bright fire was burning in the recess in the wall, and Robert thrust a spluttering torch into a bracket by the door. He bowed to Peter, and the door clanged behind him. At last he was alone.

Peter wandered restlessly round the room, examining the various objects there with tired and yawning curiosity. He would have liked to inspect the exciting things there more closely, for he was convinced that this would be his last chance. In a few minutes he would be undressed, and asleep. When he awoke, it would be to see the familiar comfort of his bedroom at Llysmeddyg.

As he struggled with the long scarlet hose, Peter felt undecided about that. It would be a pity not to see more of this strange savage world into which he had been thrust, and yet it would be a relief to be back in his own world again, where he need not worry over every move and word.

He looked round for his pyjamas. But there were none. Even young noblemen of the fourteenth century wore no pyjamas, he realized, as he tumbled into the hard bed. The torch had spluttered itself into a dull glow, and even the fire had died down to a faint gleam. Peter stared through the darkness to the grey light of the open window. He could see a star twinkling in the black sky, and he smiled drowsily.

He would see that star again tomorrow night. Only then it would be six hundred years older. His eyes shut, and he breathed evenly as a lovely feeling of languor crept over him. A log fell in the fireplace, but Peter did not stir. He was fast asleep.

7

A Medieval Manor

Peter yawned, and stretched his legs luxuriously. As he opened his eyes, and blinked, he grinned. He would have plenty to tell the vicar today. It had been a vivid and quite incredibly exciting dream.

The grin was wiped off his face. For it was not the deep-blue curtains of his bedroom that he saw, but the rough stone wall, and open gaping slit window of Carreg Cennen Castle. He was still in the round chamber of Peter de Blois.

Peter gasped, half with shock, and half with cold, for a chilly breeze was blowing in through the window. He dived back under the thick rugs, and stared wildly about him. For this was still the dream world he had seen last night. If it was a dream . . . for the first time a feeling of doubt passed through his head. And then, in a blinding flash, he realized that it was not a dream at all.

There was nothing unreal about the bare furniture of his room, the rough stools, the big chest of clothes, and row of wooden pegs hammered into the stone wall.

From outside he could hear the sounds of the waking castle, the whinny of horses, and the voices of men. They were up early, he thought, for even without his watch he could tell by the light outside that the sun had barely risen.

Quick feet sounded outside, and Robert came into the room.

'Still abed, my lord,' he said with surprise.

59

'Yes, of course,' Peter said. 'It's not time to get up yet, Robert. The sun's only just up.'

'It has been up this half-hour, my lord,' Robert said in tones of reproof. 'And you know well how the Lord Roger has a short temper for laggards in the morning.'

He started to lay out the clothes which Peter had been wearing when he had first found himself with the gauntlet in his hand.

With a groan, Peter crawled reluctantly out of the warm rugs.

'Ouch!' he yelped, as the cold breeze hit him. He had forgotten that he was not wearing pyjamas. It was cold standing there.

He grabbed the rough linen vest that Robert was holding out for him, and was soon half-dressed. There seemed to be no question of a wash this morning, and Peter yearned for the warm steam-heated bathroom of Llysmeddyg.

A sudden thought struck him.

'Where do you sleep, Robert?' he asked curiously.

'My lord!' Robert stared at him in surprise. 'On the floor of the great hall, of course, my lord.'

'Oh, yes, of course,' Peter mumbled.

On the floor of the hall! With all the rest of the inhabitants of the castle garrison, Peter realized. In the thick smelly rushes. He remembered what one of the books in Mr Evans's library had said about the habits of medieval people. He could count himself lucky to have even a truckle bed and a straw mattress.

He followed Robert down the stairs, and out into the courtyard. It was already filled with a crowd of busy people, who bobbed their heads respectfully as Peter made his way towards the steps of the hall, watching carefully to see where Robert led him. A line of armed men were drawn up by the massive gatehouse, and Peter would have liked to inspect them, but he was given no time.

'Laggard,' growled Lord Roger, as Peter slipped into his place on the dais.

He was gnawing a bone, and looked like a bad-tempered dog. He wrenched away the last piece of meat with a grunt, and hurled the bone across the hall.

'When I was a page, my son,' he said, picking up another bone, 'I would have been soundly flogged for coming down at such an hour. But then you boys are soft these days. Ach!' He bit off a hunk of meat, and chewed noisily.

Even the abbot did not seem in a good mood that morning. He was eating slowly, his eyes half shut, and occasionally he stroked his forehead. Peter began to realize that the two men had sat up late last night. A modern doctor would have prescribed a dose of bicarbonate of soda for them. Pity, Peter thought. They should have a copy of *The Times* each, as his father did in the morning, and then they could have cheered themselves up with the cricket scores.

There was plenty to eat for breakfast, cold joints, eggs, and fish. Peter chose eggs, and they were good, hard-boiled ones, and fresh. The bread was thick and coarse to his modern palate, but he could find nothing wrong with the butter. He washed the meal down with weak ale, though he would have given a great deal for a cup of hot tea.

Lord Roger had cheered up by the end of the meal, and turned to the abbot.

'You ride for Valle Crucis this morning?' he asked.

'Yes, my lord. I would have stayed at your hospitable board for another night . . . ' he shook his head in appreciation of the dinner he had eaten.

'I shall be riding over in two days with the boys,' Lord Roger said.

The Lady Marian turned to Peter, and smiled.

'My lord thinks you should learn your letters, Peter,' she said. 'And what better place than at Valle Crucis?'

The abbot beamed at him.

'We will soon have you writing,' he said. 'Brother Hugh, the master of the novices, is a wonderful teacher. He has great patience.'

Peter blinked. Learn to write! Had he forgotten how to read and write now that he was back in 1300?

'When I was a page,' rumbled Lord Roger, 'I wasted no time on such things as letters. Riding, the use of arms, and tilting, those are the accomplishments of a page. Why, even today, my Lord Abbot,' he added with pride, 'I can do no more than write my name.'

'Indeed,' said the abbot tactfully. 'But it will be useful to the boy, nevertheless. When he succeeds to the estates and manors, he will need no clerk . . . '

'I suppose so,' Lord Roger said doubtfully, and rose from the table.

They all went outside to bid farewell to the abbot. An abbot of a great monastery such as Valle Crucis was an important man, Peter realized, for both Lord Roger and the Lady Marian treated him with considerable respect. And outside, in the great courtyard of the castle, the abbot's escort was drawn up in readiness for his return journey.

It was an impressive escort, probably more for display than protection, for no robber would dare, in those superstitious days, to attack an abbot. There were half a dozen abbey servants, well armed and horsed; two monks who had accompanied the abbot, one of whom acted as his secretary, and three personal servants.

The abbot paused at the top of the steps outside the hall, and turned to thank his host and hostess. Then he lifted his hand, and they all knelt obediently while he intoned a swift Latin blessing over them. Two of his servants led forward his horse, and he was half helped, half pushed into the high saddle. He smiled at them, waved his hand, and the cavalcade moved off towards the gatehouse. Peter heard the dull echoing boom of the hooves as the horsemen crossed the wooden drawbridge beyond, and vanished from sight.

Roger turned cheerfully to his family.

'Are you riding today, my lord?' piped up small Henry, looking up anxiously at the tall figure of his father.

Lord Roger grinned down at the tiny boy.

'I am,' he said cheerfully. 'And do you want to come with me, mannikin?'

'I'm not a mannikin,' protested Henry. 'I grew an inch last year. But I would like to come with you,' he added politely, 'if it please you, sir?'

'It does please me, giant,' Lord Roger said.

Half an hour later he clattered through the gatehouse, followed by Peter, Glyndwr, and Henry. Surrounding the sheer walls of the castle was a deep V-shaped ditch, quite twenty feet deep in places. Peter examined it with interest, for there had been little trace of it in the twentieth century. It looked a formidable obstacle, but apparently Lord Roger did not think so, for he shouted for one of the sentries.

A grizzled old soldier hurried out of the guardroom. He was wearing a coat of mail, and a steel helmet.

'You called, my lord?' he asked.

'Yes, William. The ditch. The walls are crumbling there. See! Have ten men to work this morning. And clear those weeds.'

Lord Roger twitched his rein, and they trotted down the track to the road. As he followed, Peter, who was glad that he had learnt to ride in the twentieth century, wondered why Lord Roger should be so particular, even fussy, about the state of the castle ditch.

'You aren't expecting an attack, are you, my lord?' he asked politely, and a little nervously, for he was never certain what these people might think of the most innocent remark. But to his relief Lord Roger took the question seriously.

'No, Peter. But only a fool would neglect his defences here.' He shot a swift glance around to where Glyndwr was riding some ten yards behind them, and then dropped his voice. 'You never know when these Welsh chieftains might get out of hand.'

Peter's eyes opened with surprise and a certain amount of excitement. An attack on the castle would be something worth seeing.

A few minutes' riding brought them to the medieval Llanferon. There was one building only that was familiar to Peter, and that was the church, which did not seem to have changed much since he had seen it last. But the rest of the village was a disappointment. The houses were nothing but hovels to his eyes; they had no chimneys, and smoke oozed from every crack and crevice. The walls were of mud and rushes, and the only light was that which came in through the door, for windows meant glass, and that was a rare and costly item in the fourteenth century.

Lord Roger made a brisk round of his manor. He stopped to talk to the chief officials, the reeve, the hayward, or hedger, and finally the beeward, a man of some importance in those days, when the only source of sweetening came from honey.

Lord Roger's manner was curt and aloof with these men, as if there was a considerable gulf between them and a member of the de Blois family. He pulled up his horse by one man who was lounging against a tree.

'Why are you not in the fields, Sim?' he barked.

The fellow bowed, and tugged at his cap.

'If you please, your lordship,' he said nervously, 'it is my foot.'

'What ails it?' demanded Lord Roger impatiently.

'It is poisoned, my fair lord.'

'Go to the castle, then. The Lady Marian will give you some ointment.'

'Mark you, Peter,' Lord Roger said as they rode away, 'one day you will have the ordering of this manor. See that you treat these villeins aright. Sim is a bad worker at the best of times, and I care not if his foot falls off. But he will be one less in the fields, and that is what matters.'

Peter eyed Lord Roger with surprise. He was shocked at the casual, even callous attitude of a man who with his own family had seemed a kindly person.

'They are but animals, you see,' Lord Roger added carelessly, 'and stupid ones at that.'

They rode round the fields, of which there were three, each one of many acres, divided into long strips, and each strip bounded by a raised baulk of turf. Glyndwr started to ask questions, using words such as 'boon work', which were quite strange to Peter. But he gathered that the villeins worked on the lord's strips three days a week, instead of paying rent, and that this work was called boon work.

'Wouldn't it be better if you paid them?' Peter asked, when Lord Roger was complaining that it was difficult to make the men work on his land, for they were always anxious to farm their own strips first, which was natural enough.

'Some of them stay away, if they wish,' Lord Roger said. 'But they pay me, Peter. Two silver shillings a year, two baskets of eggs, and two chickens. With the money I hire men to do their work.'

Peter wished he knew something about modern farming, for even to his amateur eyes this manor was not very well farmed. The ploughs were clumsy implements that barely scratched the surface of the ground, and the cattle that he saw were small and bony. They stopped by some pigs, or so Lord Roger called them. Peter looked at them with astonishment.

They were thin and hairy animals, with a back of stiff bristles, dangerous looking beasts with long pointed snouts and sharp fangs.

'The cattle are poor,' grumbled Lord Roger, pointing to some painfully thin cows near them. 'But what can you expect when you have to kill off most of them each winter.'

'Why?' Peter asked in surprise.

'What is there to feed them on?'

Peter knew the answer to that, and out it came before he had time to check the quick thought.

'Why not give them turnips?' he said.

'What?' Lord Roger eyed him with a puzzled expression. 'On what, Peter? I have never heard the word.'

'Oh . . . er . . . I was thinking of something else, my lord.' Peter flushed and mumbled. Turnips were not invented, or whatever the expression was with food, he remembered, until many hundreds of years later.

Fortunately Lord Roger's attention was distracted by some other point he wished to discuss with the reeve, the chief officer and overseer of the manor, and he did not notice Peter's embarrassment.

On their way back they halted by the church, and Lord Roger went inside to see the priest. With some curiosity, Peter followed him. The nave had not changed much for he recognized some of the stained-glass windows. But the walls were covered with brightly coloured paintings, crude and vigorous, showing what would happen to sinners when they arrived in Hell. Not very encouraging,

Peter thought, but then they were not supposed to be, he decided.

Whilst Lord Roger was in conversation with the priest, Peter hurried up the nave in the direction of the chancel and the choir stalls. There was one particular thing he wished to see. He reached the stalls, slowed down and stared at the wall on the left, half dreading what he was going to see.

His worst fears were realized. For there was no brass to Peter de Blois. That was still to come. And when? The Peter de Blois, who stood there with the blood draining from his face, shivered and then turned and walked quickly out of the church into the fresh spring air and the sun.

He was still in a state of deep depression when they trotted across the drawbridge, and pulled up at the foot of the steps leading into the hall.

8

THE LONGBOW

The midday meal was not an exciting one, and to Peter it seemed still very early in the day. But then he remembered that they had all been up since dawn. In those days when lights were crude and expensive, he realized that people must make the best use of the daylight. The food was cold meat, salted fish, a few vegetables, followed by a huge fruit pie.

'What are you doing this afternoon?' Glyndwr asked him abruptly. It was almost the first remark he had addressed to Peter.

'I don't quite know,' Peter said, wishing that this boy really was Gwyn. They could talk then, and try to find some way out of the extraordinary position in which Peter had found himself.

Lord Roger settled the question of the afternoon's amusement.

'I am going down to the butts,' he said. 'Peter, you will come with me. It is high time you learnt how to handle a longbow.'

The prospect of seeing medieval archers actually at practice roused Peter from his state of gloom. This was the heyday of the longbow, and he wondered frantically if the battle of Crécy had yet been fought, for he was still vague about the exact date. But if Henry was to be killed at Poitiers they must be at the beginning of the century, for dates were Peter's strong point. They stuck in his head like glue. Poitiers was fought about 1350, and Crécy ten years before that. They must be about the year 1330 now, he reckoned.

Peter was still wrestling with his dates when they reached the butts which were set up by the stream below the castle. The targets were thick trusses of straw marked with a white splodge in the centre. Some were about a hundred yards away from the firing point, though there were others at a shorter range.

He watched the practice with delight, for not only was it a new experience for him, but it was a beautiful sight as well. There was the graceful stance of the archer, the curve of the great bows, the deep twang of the string, and the thin high-pitched whistle of the shaft as it hurtled towards its target.

Old William, the grizzled veteran who had been in command of the gatehouse guard that morning, was in charge of the practice. The bowmen, Peter noticed, were Welshmen, for they were chattering in their own language.

'We shall have a goodly company of bowmen, my lord,' old William said, as Lord Roger strolled up to him.

'Good! Did you bring the small bow for Lord Peter?'

William nodded, and picked up a small bow. To Peter it seemed an immense size. William held it against him, as if measuring it.

'Too short, my lord,' he said.

'But how can you tell?' Peter asked.

'It must be the same height as yourself, my lord.' He tried two other longer bows, until he found one that fitted Peter's height. Then he started his lesson.

'Sideways to the butt, my lord. Shoulders up, head back.' He pushed Peter into position. 'The left foot forward. So!'

He handed over the bow.

'Fingers of the left hand below the binding,' he went on. 'Grip hard! Now, the first and second fingers on the shaft. Now for the art of pulling.'

He closed his big hand over Peter's, and showed him how to grasp the string with the fingers of the right hand, leaving the first and second fingers to hold the shaft of the arrow.

'Now, pull back to the ear, my lord,' he said.

Peter tugged. The string came back, but it was hard work. He braced himself, and hauled with all his strength. The thick arc of the bow creaked as he tugged at the thick greased string.

'Stand upright, my lord,' cried old William. 'Do not bend forward to the bow.'

Peter's face went purple with his efforts, until the string came slowly back to his ear.

'Good! Again! Again!'

There followed five minutes of really hard work as Peter wrestled with his bow, merely practising the art of pulling. He found that once he learnt the knack of standing bolt upright, it was a little easier, but his arm and shoulders were aching at the end of that first practice.

'Now, watch me, my lord,' William said.

He picked up his bow, a monster of a weapon, nearly six feet from tip to tip, with an immensely thick shaft, tapering slightly towards each end. He took up his stance, slid forwards his left foot, and carefully placed a thin goose-feathered shaft into place. As he raised the bow, so he began to pull, with one single graceful effort, though to Peter there seemed very little effort about the way in which the great bow bent.

There was no pause for an aim. As William's hand reached his ear, so he let go. The powerful string twanged, a deep resonant note, and the arrow hissed away. It rose gracefully in the air, reached the full height of its flight, then plunged down towards the hundred-yard target. There was a loud 'clock', and there was the goose-feathered end quivering wildly.

Lord Roger smiled, and William patted his great bow with affection.

'Now, my lord,' he said, turning to Peter. 'Fit the shaft. Notch it. So! Fingers behind the feathers. Now, pull back!'

Peter strained away, one set of fingers straining on the shaft, the others tugging at the string.

'Let go as the shaft comes up to the mark,' William said.

With a grunt, Peter gave a final tug, and let go. The arrow swooped up with a wavering flight, and then buried itself in the turf yards away from the twenty-yard target at which he had aimed. It had seemed impossible to miss it.

Old William smiled patiently at Peter's groan of disgust.

'Practice, my lord,' he said. 'When I was younger than you I had to stand for hours, just holding the bow. And if my arm wavered, my father would strike my hand with a stick.'

Peter tried again.

'Pull as you come up to the aim,' William said. 'No, my lord, your eye on the mark, not on the arrow tip.'

Peter grinned, despite the effort of pulling back. For one fleeting moment there flashed through his mind the cry of his cricket coach at school. 'Keep your eye on the ball, Staunton.' That seemed a pretty general rule, to keep your eye on the ball, playing cricket, golf, or even when using a longbow.

He watched the butt ahead, sensed that the shaft was at the right height, and let go. There was a much more satisfying twang this time. But he had aimed too low. The arrow dropped just short, and buried itself in the turf, the feathers shivering as if in derision at his efforts.

'That's better,' Lord Roger said.

Peter shook his head crossly. It was infuriating to think that he, who had shot an airgun hundreds of times, could not even hit a target twenty yards away. These people watching him now would have fallen flat on their faces with fright if he had produced that gun.

He took another shaft from William. If he broke his arm in the process, he would hit the target this time.

'Make allowance for the distance, my lord,' William said.

Peter notched the arrow carefully, and nodded. Elevation, that was the answer to all shooting.

Peter could see his left hand rising slowly above the level of the target. Twang! With his mouth half open, Peter watched the flight. The arrow plunged down, and then 'clock' came the satisfying sound from the target as the arrow plunged into the straw.

Peter practised hard for the next half-hour, and his aim improved rapidly. By that time his arm was aching, and the muscles of his back felt as if they were breaking. But he had enjoyed himself.

'How far can you shoot an arrow, William?' he asked.

The old soldier smiled and shook his head.

'Once . . . ' he smiled ruefully. 'I am too old now, my lord. But Evan Ap Rees here can pull a long shaft. Over two hundred and fifty paces is his best.'

'Bid him show us,' Lord Roger said.

William called to the young archer. He was a tall, dark-haired man, with broad shoulders and bulging arm muscles. He grinned with delight at the chance of showing his skill, and took up his stance. His bow was so thick that Peter wondered how any man could draw it back even a few inches. Evan selected a shaft with great care, discarded three that William handed him, looked intently at the feathers, trimmed them, weighed the arrow in his hands to feel the balance, and then drew on the heavy leather shooting gauntlet for his left hand.

He notched the arrow, slid forward his left foot, and began to draw. Despite his massive build, there was no sign of clumsiness about him. On the contrary, he was a figure of simple grace. Back came the massive bow in a broad arc, with an effortless ease that made Peter grin with envious delight. The tip of the arrow pointed well up in the air now, to gain the maximum of elevation, and as the hand reached the ear, Evan let go.

With a deep musical twang, the shaft screamed into the air. All heads went up to follow it, and then down again as it began to fall. Pushed by the slight following breeze it seemed to gain momentum as it shot down and hit the ground at an immense distance away.

'Gosh!' muttered Peter in very un-medieval language.

'Three hundred paces, I warrant,' Lord Roger said. 'Bid a man pace it, William.'

One of the archers walked off, and they could hear him counting the paces aloud. He turned, and cupped his hands to shout.

'Two hundred and seventy paces, my lord!'

'Good! good!' Lord Roger said. 'It was a following wind, but a fair shoot.' He fumbled in his pouch and threw a coin to the grinning Evan.

Peter walked back to the castle with Lord Roger. He was happier now than he had felt at any time since his arrival. He had, indeed, come to the sensible conclusion that it was no use fighting this dream, if dream it was. He might as well make the most of it, and gain as much pleasure and interest as he could from all the strange and fascinating sights around him.

He bathed and dressed for dinner in the great hall. The Lady Marian, Lord Roger, Glyndwr, and Henry were already in the sitting room above the hall. Peter had by this time learned its proper name, the 'solar'.

Lord Roger was in a cheerful mood, and the Lady Marian asked him about his longbow shooting. She smiled, and patted him affectionately.

'I might have done far worse in the way of parents,' Peter reflected, as he went across to the deep window seat where Henry was playing.

He had two figures of wood; they were joined cleverly at the arms and legs, and were dressed in armour. Henry was holding them with strings, and their feet were weighed with tiny pieces of lead to make them stand. Peter took one end of the strings, and as he pulled, the two soldiers jerked their wooden swords, and in a second were fighting madly, to the accompaniment of shouts from little Henry. Peter was surprised to find such an ingenious toy in the fourteenth century, and he played happily with Henry until the trumpets sounded for dinner.

Lord Roger was hungry, and turned anxiously to the Lady Marian as he sat down in his huge arm chair with its elaborately carved back.

'I have asked them to prepare your favourite pork liver, my lord,' the Lady Marian said.

Lord Roger rubbed his hands with delight.

'Well spiced, I hope,' he said.

The Lady Marian laughed. 'You had best come to the kitchen and see.'

'Indeed I will,' and Lord Roger jumped up.

Peter thought that this was a chance not to be missed, and he followed them down the hall, and through the screen at the far end. Here they were met by the steward, a portly and important man, responsible for all the food and clothing of the castle, and the accommodation of guests. The equivalent, in fact, of the modern butler.

He bowed with difficulty, for his waist measurements were enormous, and Peter came to the conclusion that he must take the food side of his duties very seriously.

'The Lord Roger wishes to see the preparation of the pork livers,' the Lady Marian said.

'I have this moment seen the cook, my lady,' the steward said in a deep fruity voice that matched his appearance. His face was red after the exertion of bowing, and he rubbed his hands together furiously. 'But, come, my lord, and see for yourself.'

The kitchen was an immense place, with a vaulted stone ceiling and a central space to allow the smoke to escape. There were no less than three fireplaces, and in front of one were several spits—long spikes, on which joints of meat were skewered. Boys were turning them slowly, pausing now and then to pour basting gravy over the meat. It was hot work, and the perspiration was streaming off their faces.

'Now, my lord,' the steward said, raising his voice above the terrific clatter and noise. 'We have taken the pork liver, pounded it well, and put to it ground pepper, cloves, cinnamon, and currants.'

'What, no saffron?' Lord Roger said anxiously.

The steward rounded angrily on the unfortunate cook.

'No saffron for my lord's pork liver balls?' he demanded furiously.

'I shall use that to colour the balls after roasting them, my lord,' the cook said hastily.

'Good,' Lord Roger murmured. 'Proceed, good steward.'

'Yes, my lord. Then we shall make the pork into balls, wet them well in whites of eggs, place them in boiling water, and let them seethe. Then spit and roast them well. Then take parsley, grind it with eggs, of course, my lord,' the steward smacked his lips, and rubbed his hands furiously, 'then strain them, and colour with saffron.'

He looked anxiously at Lord Roger for his approval.

'Excellent,' Lord Roger said heartily.

'I should think so, too,' Peter said to himself, as he tried to take in all the details of this incredible dish.

Dinner passed off in the slow ceremonious way as that of the previous night. The trumpets sounded for each course, and Peter waited on Lord Roger with the various dishes, and helped him to wine. The pork liver balls were produced by the steward in person, with the anxious face of the cook hovering in the background. To Peter they looked very much like oranges in appearance, due to the saffron colouring. He learnt afterwards that their proper name was 'pomme de orynge' so he was not far wrong.

Lord Roger was in a cheerful mood by the end of dinner. He had eaten an enormous meal, and the liver balls had been superb, so he had assured the steward. He was about to call for the castle minstrel to entertain them when a sudden and unusual silence fell on the crowded tables in the centre of the hall.

'What is this?' demanded Lord Roger.

'It is Blodwen Rees, my lord,' the steward whispered in his ear.

'The witch?' Lord Roger muttered uneasily. He crossed himself hurriedly. 'How did she enter? I will have word with the gateward in the morning.'

The Lady Marian leant forward.

'It is I who am to blame,' she said. 'The old crone brought me some healing herbs this afternoon.'

'But she has the devil's eye,' Lord Roger protested. 'You do wrong, Marian. If I had my way, I would let the church drive her out of the manor with bell, book, and candle.'

The Lady Marian tried to reassure him, but he would not listen. And he was too late, for a bent old woman, with white hair and wrinkled face, had already approached the dais.

'You need have no fear, my lord,' she said, grinning at the half-scared Lord Roger. 'I have come to thank the Lady Marian for her gift of some salted fish.'

'Then thank her and begone,' growled Lord Roger.

The old woman chuckled, and looked round the faces at the high table. Her dark eyes fell on Peter. With his twentieth-century upbringing, he was a little amused and scornful of Lord Roger's superstitious fear, but as those piercing eyes bored into him, he shifted uneasily on his stool.

'A fine son, my lord,' she said. 'Shall I tell you his fortune?'

Lord Roger looked at her with sudden interest.

'Can you tell the future, witch?' he asked.

She cackled, and nodded her white head.

'Cross my hand with silver first, my young lord,' she said, pointing at Peter.

'Throw her a groat, Peter,' Lord Roger said. His interest was thoroughly aroused by this time.

Peter opened his purse, and fumbled inside with the unfamiliar coins. Lady Marian bent over, and pulled out a small silver coin, which Peter handed to the witch. She spat on it, and then tucked it away in the depths of her filthy cloak. Then she came forward, and caught hold of Peter's shrinking hand, turning the palm upwards.

'Look upon the water, my lord,' she said, pointing to the big bowl of water by his side.

There was a tense silence at the table. Lord Roger and the Lady Marian craned forward curiously.

'Think of your greatest desire, my lord,' the old woman said.

Peter wrinkled his forehead. He thought that the witch was a fraud, and wondered what faked mumbo-jumbo she would produce for the entertainment of Lord Roger.

But at the words of the witch, his thoughts went instinctively to the familiar things of his life, the common sights of the modern world, a busy city street, an aeroplane, the shops, the tall buildings, a steamer, a railway engine tearing along . . .

There was a shrill scream of high-pitched terror from the old witch. She snatched her hand away. Her dark eyes were fixed on Peter with an expression of real dread. Then she backed away slowly, her skinny hands up, shaking uncontrollably.

'Who are you, in the fiend's name?' she muttered. 'What strange visions do you conjure up in the water? They are not of this world! I cannot read the lines of your hand. You are from . . . ' She screamed again. 'You are of the devil!'

There was a deep silence over all the hall. Peter was staring at her with a fear as great as hers. But from Lord Roger there came a roar of fury. He stood up, pushing back his heavy chair so violently that it toppled over, and fell with a crash that resounded loudly through the silent hall. His face was dark with anger.

'Begone, you foul witch!' he roared. 'Out! Out! this minute, before I set the dogs upon you!'

He picked up a heavy tankard from the table, and as the old woman cackled derisively, her sudden fear gone, Lord Roger let out a bellow of furious rage. He hurled the tankard at her head with a gesture of blind superstitious panic.

The tankard sailed past her head. She turned, and ran down the hall. As she went, the terrified people at the tables drew back from her as if she were suffering from the plague.

In the dead silence that followed Lord Roger's wild shout, they heard the squeal of the great door as it turned on its hinges, and then a loud defiant clang, and she was gone.

9

FALCONRY

As Peter took his seat on the dais at breakfast the next morning, he looked around him nervously. Surely the others must have realized the meaning of that appalling incident at dinner? That sinister old woman had sensed that he was different from all the other people in the hall, and by this time Lord Roger at least, if not the Lady Marian too, must have guessed it as well.

But Peter need not have worried. For he had not realized how great was the childish superstition of medieval people. To them, that old crone was merely the possessor of the Evil Eye; she had been trying to place a spell on Peter. Unpleasant, no doubt, but not the kind of thing to talk about; something to be forgotten as soon as possible. And to Peter's tremendous relief, it was never mentioned again, in his hearing at any rate.

He finished his breakfast of eggs, butter and bread, and sour ale, and then wandered out into the courtyard of the castle. He had given up all hope of making friends with Glyndwr; the Welsh boy had relapsed into a mood of sullen hostility, and rarely opened his mouth. He spent most of his time with his Welsh servants, and as they talked in their own language, no one was any the wiser.

It was pleasant in the courtyard. Spring was early that year, and Peter sat on the stone steps, and watched the busy scene with fascinated eyes. Lord Roger was inspecting the guard on the gatehouse, and old William was detailing the men to their various posts on the walls.

Peter was beginning to realize that Carreg Cennen was never left unguarded at any time of the day or night.

Lord Roger strolled up; by his side was a man who carried a large bird on his wrist. Its head was covered with a closely fitting hood, and he was stroking it at regular intervals with a feather. Peter had seen this before. There were several men in the castle who appeared to have no other occupation than to wander around with birds on their wrists. Peter knew enough from his reading to guess that they were falconers, for hawking was one of the favourite pastimes of the Middle Ages.

'Your goshawk is fully trained now, my lord,' the falconer said, as he came up to Peter.

'This one?' Peter asked, pointing to the bird.

'Oh, no, my lord. This is a haggard peregrine falcon. He will not be loosed for many days yet.'

Peter tried to conceal his ignorance of the subject, but he was anxious to learn all he could. Fortunately the falconer saw nothing unusual in Peter's lack of knowledge.

'I am going to the mews, my lord,' he said. 'Would you care to see your goshawk? The Lord Roger is hawking today, and you should take your bird, too.'

Peter nodded eagerly, and followed the man across to the far corner of the courtyard, where the mews stood, a long lean-to shed of wood. As he went, he tried to remember the little he had read about falconry, but it was not a great deal. He knew that falcons and hawks were trained to fly and catch other birds in mid-air, but exactly how it was done, he had only the faintest of notions.

The mews was a long low room, dark and narrow. Against the wall on one side was a padded perch about five feet from the ground, and sitting on this was a row of motionless birds. They were all wearing leather hoods, and sat there without the slightest flicker of movement, as if petrified.

The falconer put down the bird he had been carrying, and then picked up some small pieces of raw meat. It seemed part of his duties to teach Peter the art of hawking, for he gave a short running commentary on what he was doing.

'Watch, my lord,' he said, 'these are freshly trapped tiercels.'

'What's a tiercel?' Peter came to the conclusion that he might as well show complete ignorance, for he would learn nothing otherwise.

'A tiercel is the male bird, my lord. An eyas is a hawk trained from the nest, caught young, you see, whilst the haggard is one caught wild when it is fully grown.'

The falconer, whom Peter had heard of as John of the Falcon, took a feather, brushed the legs of one of the birds, and caused him to bend down his head. Then he snapped up the meat in his sharp beak.

'They are not yet trained to feed with the hood off,' John said. He gave a low whistle each time the birds swallowed the meat, and Peter noticed that the second bird bent down immediately he heard the whistle.

'Ah, he is coming to nicely,' John remarked with satisfaction. 'I will unhood him tomorrow.'

He fed the other tiercels in the same way, and then went into another room in the mews. This was much lighter, and the birds seemed tamer. John unhooded them, and as he called them by name, they jumped on to his outstretched fist, and then swallowed the little titbits of meat. They were beautiful creatures, fully grown peregrine falcons, as John explained, and were Lord Roger's own birds, well trained, and veteran hunters.

'And this is Jehanne, your goshawk, my lord,' John said. 'Feed her yourself, and she will become used to your handling.'

He pulled a soft leather glove over Peter's left hand, and gave him a piece of meat.

'Put your hand under her talons, my lord.'

With some hesitation, Peter did as he was told. The goshawk hopped off her perch, and clung tightly to Peter's gloved fingers. John took her hood off gently, and she blinked in the fresh morning sunlight.

Peter forgot his nervousness in his delight that such a lovely bird was his. Jehanne had a broad tail, barred with streaks of black, and her white breast was covered with blackish grey spots.

'Whistle,' murmured John.

Peter gave a soft low whistle. Jehanne dropped her handsome head, and nibbled daintily at the meat in Peter's fingers. Then she looked up at him from fierce eyes and blinked, as if in thanks. Peter grinned down at her with pride, and stroked her gently. He knew from what John had been telling him that despite their fierce appearance, falcons and goshawks became very attached to their owners, and Jehanne seemed to have taken a liking to him already.

'Good! good! my lord,' John said. 'Now! Let us take her out, and see if you have forgotten all the lessons I gave you. You must not disgrace yourself if you ride with the Lord Roger today.'

Peter was afraid that he had forgotten all the lessons, but he followed John out of the mews, and down to the field below the castle. Jehanne clung tightly to his hand, but Peter was quite used to that now. He was far too delighted at being the owner of such a magnificent hawk.

In the field John explained what they were going to do. He showed Peter the 'lure': a kind of big tassel on the end of a piece of string. If held upside down, the skirt of the tassel fell away, and revealed a small chunk of meat fastened to a pin.

'I will go a hundred paces away, my lord,' John said. 'When I shout, do you hold up your hand, and I will show the lure. Then cast off Jehanne.'

He showed Peter how to unleash the hawk. Round her leg was a thin strap called the 'jess', and this was fastened to a swivel of silver, the varvels. If Peter pulled out a small piece of wood, known as the button, the hawk was freed instantly.

John walked away, and then stopped at the agreed distance. Up went his hand, and he shouted. Jehanne had already been freed from her hood, and was quivering with excitement, and as Peter pulled out the button, and held his gloved hand in the air, the hawk took off, her powerful wings shooting her up into the air. She was, as John of the Falcon had said, well trained, for after one dive she made straight for the lure. After half an hour's more practice with Peter holding the lure, John declared himself satisfied.

'She will do us credit this afternoon,' he said.

'Are you coming hawking with us?' Peter asked.

'His lordship would not go without me,' John said proudly.

They set off immediately after the midday meal, Lord Roger on a powerful black horse, and the Lady Marian on a lighter mare.

'Where is Glyndwr?' the Lady Marian asked, as she prepared to mount into her high saddle.

'He has gone riding with his servants, my lady,' Robert said.

'Riding? Where?' Lord Roger looked round sharply.

Robert shook his head helplessly.

'It matters not,' Lord Roger growled, and he twitched his reins impatiently.

They clattered under the frowning gatehouse, and made for the great open heath some miles from the castle, where,

as Peter gathered from the conversation between Lord
Roger and John of the Falcon, they had found good sport
on previous occasions.

It was a sunny spring day, with a clear blue sky flecked
with fleecy white clouds. The gorse on the heath was in
full bloom, a glorious stretch of colour, and the air, as they
cantered over the soft turf, was clean and fresh.

Peter wriggled in his saddle with sudden joy and
excitement. He was feeling happier now than he had been
for some days, and as he looked round the beautiful
countryside, he began to realize that the twentieth century
had not introduced every possible improvement on
medieval times, as he had sometimes imagined. England
was a country with a tiny population in 1300, and here in
the centre of Wales, a thinly populated area at the best of
times, there were many miles of open country, bare of
even the slightest trace of human beings.

His eyes fell on the three riders ahead. The Lord Roger
in his brilliantly coloured clothes, his magnificent surcoat
with the great silver gauntlet proudly emblazoned on the
breast, a long sword dangling from his belt, and the superb
peregrine falcon perched proudly on his wrist, was a
figure straight from the most fanciful of all Peter's dreams
of medieval glory and pageantry.

The Lady Marian, too, in her beautiful riding dress, was
a mass of dazzling colour, and while John of the Falcon
was more soberly clothed, both made Peter tingle with
delight. The whole cavalcade might have jumped straight
from some lavish Technicolor film, if Peter had not looked
down, and seen his own bright cote-hardie and hose, and
the fierce goshawk on his wrist.

'Make for the pool,' Lord Roger called out, as he swung
to the left, and galloped along a narrow track.

Peter came back to the fourteenth century with a jolt,
and went over the lesson in hawking that John of the

Falcon had given him that morning. Falcons, he knew now, could be flown at many different types of quarry, but the heron provided the finest sport, because of its tremendous speed. It was no match for the falcon if caught rising from a river or a pond, but once well on the wing, and high in the air, it was a different proposition. It was not considered sporting to set a falcon on to a sitting bird, and a heron 'on passage' that is, flying from its nest to a pond or brook, was the ideal quarry of the medieval falconer.

When they reached the large pool in the centre of the heath, a likely spot for herons to visit on passage, the horses were pulled up, and the falcons unhooded. A pair of them had been brought out, for it was the fashion to fly a 'cast' of them at a heron, that is, a pair at a time.

They were magnificent birds, with black heads, slatey grey wings of great strength, white throats, and chests streaked with black bars. In vivid contrast to these colours was the bright yellow of their legs, and indeed, they presented a wonderful picture of vigour and grace, as they peered up into the blue sky with their fierce eyes.

There was a pause of some minutes, and the riders searched the sky for a sign of the quarry.

'A heron, a heron!' shouted John of the Falcon. He pointed to a tiny speck in the sky.

'You are right,' Lord Roger said. 'A heron on passage!'

To Peter, it was a small black dot in the air, but he stiffened in his saddle, becoming aware of the suppressed excitement in the others.

'Wait! wait! Slip your falcon when I call, John,' Lord Roger called out.

It was advice wasted on such an experienced falconer like John. The falcons had seen the quarry now, and were straining at their leashes, the tiny bells on their feet tinkling loudly.

'Loose!' bellowed Lord Roger. 'Loose!'

He pulled out the button, and flung his bird into the air. John did the same, and the two birds shot up into the sky. The heron was about a hundred yards away now, at a considerable height, and moving at a tremendous speed. The falcons made a circle, as if to spot their prey, and then began to climb in tight circles, and almost perpendicularly, as it seemed to Peter.

Lord Roger let out a hoarse shout of encouragement, shook his bridle and thundered across the heath, his head back, and his eyes on the birds above. The others followed him at a wild gallop, climbed the slope on the farther side of the pool, and hurtled along the level ground.

Peter allowed his horse to pick its own route, which it seemed quite capable of doing, and concentrated on the chase overhead. The falcons were still well below the heron, but were climbing fast.

'They have him,' yelled Lord Roger. 'They are above, John!'

It was true. One falcon had risen above the heron, which by this time had seen the dreaded falcons. He, too, was climbing rapidly, in even smaller circles than his pursuers, but they more than made up for that with their greater strength and flying power.

The first falcon seemed to pause, then dropped like a stone towards the quarry. But the heron had seen the move. It swerved desperately, and the falcon, unable to check his terrible dive, fell past, missing by a matter of inches.

'Brave heron!' howled Lord Roger in delight at the skill of the quarry. He pulled his horse round a clump of gorse bushes with a wrist of iron, ducked his head hastily to avoid the overhanging branches of a tree, and then spurred on frantically, whilst the others tried a little more cautiously to follow his furious pace.

Meanwhile, the first falcon had whipped out to the right, and had started to climb again. But it was too late. A shout of delight from Lord Roger, John, and the Lady Marian showed that the second falcon had risen above the heron, which had accelerated in one last desperate burst for freedom.

'He swoops!' and down went the peregrine falcon like a jet fighter plane in a power dive.

'They bind, they bind!' shouted all three in a chorus of wild excitement, in which Peter joined, completely thrilled now by this wonderful sport.

The second falcon had dropped on to its quarry, and had seized it with its great talons. Both birds plunged to the ground, entwined in that fierce death grapple, and then crashed into the undergrowth about fifty yards from the madly pursuing riders.

Lord Roger pulled up his horse so suddenly that it reared up on its hind legs like a ballet dancer, whilst John jumped down from his saddle, and ran to the birds.

The heron was lying motionless, still tightly gripped by the falcon. The second peregrine was standing a few feet away. Peter noticed the dagger-like bill of the heron, as John separated the birds, and he wondered it had not made more use of such a formidable weapon to fight off the falcons.

'Couldn't he have spiked the falcons in mid-air with that bill?' he asked.

John shook his head.

'No, my lord. He depends on his wings. I have heard stories of herons beating off falcons, but I have never seen it. On the ground, maybe, and that's why a wise falcon, such as Mall here, will loose her quarry just before she reaches the ground, and then bind on again when it's safe.'

He pulled off the long plume of feathers from the back of the dead heron's head, and handed them to Lord Roger.

'You have the trophy, Peter,' Lord Roger said, and he bent over and pinned the feather in Peter's surcoat.

'Can I try Jehanne now?' Peter asked eagerly.

'Indeed you can, Peter. Tell me, John, shall we fly her from the hood, or should she wait on?'

Peter had learnt about these two methods of hawking from John that morning. The falcons were usually flown from the hood, that is, from the falconer's wrist, but the shorter winged hawks, such as Peter's goshawk, were first loosed, and when they had reached a sufficient height in the air, dogs were put in to flush out any suitable game on the ground. The hawk, hovering above, was said to be 'waiting on'.

'Wait on, my lord,' John said decisively. 'She is fresh yet to field work.'

They rode over to some trees and deep undergrowth, where there was a good chance of finding some game. The large shaggy dogs were whistled up—uncouth, clumsy beasts to Peter's eyes, more used to the pedigree breeds of the twentieth century. Still, they knew their work, for they moved instantly into the undergrowth.

'Loose Jehanne,' Lord Roger said.

Peter was almost as excited as Jehanne. He slipped off the hood, pulled out the button, and held up his hand. Jehanne took off immediately with a whirr from her powerful wings. She climbed at a tremendous rate, until she was nothing but a speck in the sky. But Peter noticed that she kept well over the dogs, as if she knew exactly what they were doing, as of course she did.

'There were some woodcock here last year,' Lord Roger said, his eyes on the dogs. 'They show fine sport for a goshawk.'

There was a series of excited barks from the dogs.

'Flushed out!' shouted John. 'A brace of woodcock, my lord!'

The woodcock flew frantically out of the trees, and started to climb, flying down wind.

'Jehanne, Jehanne!' yelled Peter in his excitement, as if the hawk could hear and understand him.

'Never fear, my lord,' muttered John. 'See how she waits up wind, and will make a down-wind stoop.'

The riders started to follow the quarry. Jehanne had seen it. She turned, wheeled, and dived. She dropped at what seemed an incredible speed, and caught up with the lumbering woodcock like an express train overhauling a goods engine.

It was a superbly timed dive. No fighter plane could have improved on it. Without a second's delay she selected her quarry, and hurtled down. Out went her hind talon. It struck the woodcock with deadly accuracy, and the bird dropped headlong to the ground. Behind it there came the trail of feathers to mark the death-blow he had received.

'Good bird, good bird!' Lord Roger shouted. 'Indeed, John, you have done well. I have seldom seen a better trained goshawk.'

Jehanne had followed her quarry down, and was sitting on the turf beside it as Peter galloped up, flushed and delighted. As he held out his gauntleted hand, Jehanne hopped up, and glanced at him from her fierce eyes, as if expecting praise. Peter crowed over her, and stroked her gently.

They hawked for another hour. The peregrines were cast again, and brought down several woodcock, much to the delight of the Lady Marian. It did not take Peter long to realize, from what she said, that hawking was not only a sport in those days. It was an essential means of varying the menu of salted meat, salted fish, and heavily spiced food which was the main diet of the winter in the fourteenth century.

As they turned for home, the dogs started barking furiously in the gorse.

'Rabbits, my lord,' John said. 'Shall we fly Jehanne?'

Peter had already unleashed the goshawk, and she shot up to wait on as before. A rabbit hurtled out into the open, rushing over the short turf at full speed.

'Tally ho!' yelled Peter, forgetting where he was, but the others were too engrossed to notice his strange expression.

Peter looked up hopefully. Surely Jehanne would never see the rabbit from that height. But he had forgotten the amazing sight possessed by hawks. Down she swooped at a terrific speed, flying low over the unfortunate rabbit like a bolt from the sky. By the time the riders had reached the spot it was all over, and Jehanne was sitting on the ground, a dead rabbit at her feet.

'A magnificent hawk,' Lord Roger said, clapping John of the Falcon on the back. 'Peter, you may give John a cup of my special malmsey wine at dinner tonight. See to it, for he has trained your bird well.'

They rode home in high spirits, for it had been a very good day's hawking. Peter was filled with happiness, and as he saw the grey frowning towers of Carreg Cennen appear over the hill, he felt for the first time that he was going home.

By his side, Lord Roger was eagerly discussing with the Lady Marian some tasty methods of cooking the woodcock and the rabbit. It would be a change from the meat which they would have had for dinner.

As they rode over the brow of the hill, Peter saw some horsemen come into sight from the hills on the left.

'That's Glyndwr,' he said.

Lord Roger looked up quickly, and reined in his horse.

'Do you ride on, Marian,' he said. 'I will wait.' There was an unusually grim expression on his face but it had completely disappeared by the time Glyndwr approached them.

'You have been far?' Lord Roger asked casually.

'Oh, no, my lord,' Glyndwr said quickly. He glanced at Lord Roger with an uneasy sidelong look which Peter did not like. 'We have been as far as Cwm Feron.'

Lord Roger's dark eyebrows shot up, but he made no comment.

'It is a pleasant ride,' Glyndwr said. 'Did you have a good day's hawking, my lord?'

'Very good,' Lord Roger said curtly. 'I am pleased you enjoyed the ride, Glyndwr. You took the mountain road?'

Glyndwr nodded. Lord Roger said nothing, but as he turned away, Peter noticed that he was frowning.

They dismounted at the foot of the steps outside the hall. Glyndwr bowed to the Lady Marian, and strode off to his room in the tower above the gatehouse. Lord Roger watched him go, pulling off his gauntlets slowly, his brows creased in thought.

'I distrust him,' he growled.

'Why?' asked Peter curiously. He felt the same, but his dislike of Glyndwr was instinctive, and he had guessed that Lord Roger had some definite reason, gained from what Glyndwr had said or done that afternoon.

'Why?' echoed Lord Roger. 'It is simple. He could not have reached Cwm Feron this afternoon.'

'But it lies only a few miles over the hill,' the Lady Marian said, as puzzled as Peter was by the remark.

'As you say, Marian, it does.' Lord Roger tugged at his long determined chin irritably. 'But the bridge over the river is down. It was washed away three days ago. William reported it to me yesterday. And, as you know, it is impossible to cross the river unless you use the bridge. The current is too strong for any horse. So wherever that young Welsh chief went today, it was not to Cwm Feron. He is lying.'

'But why should he lie?' Peter asked.

Lord Roger walked slowly up the flight of shallow steps, and paused by the great doors leading into the hall.

'That is what I would like to know,' he said thoughtfully. 'I wonder . . . I wonder,' he muttered to himself.

10

THE EDUCATION OF A PAGE

For Peter, in the days that followed, there was no lack of variety, for he was kept busy by both the Lord Roger and the Lady Marian in the duties and education considered suitable then for a page and the son of a nobleman.

Peter had once thought that his twentieth-century learning would have been far superior to anything that a medieval boy might have acquired. He could read, of course, which was unusual in the fourteenth century, and he had learnt some mathematics and science. Those subjects were taught in the few grammar schools that were being started in the towns of those days, and the monasteries too, acted as schools. But Peter, as a young nobleman, was not expected to learn such subjects, as the Lord Roger told him.

Lord Roger himself was astonishingly ignorant, by Peter's standard. But he had more important things to do, he told Peter, than to pore over dull parchments, and if there was any writing to be done, then there was a special clerk in the castle to do it. As long as the Manor Roll was kept, and the tale of work by the villeins, then Roger was satisfied. He could go off to his hunting and hawking. As for reading, books were rarities, for there was no printing then, of course, and each book had to be copied out slowly and laboriously by hand.

So Peter learnt other subjects. John of the Falcon taught him the art of falconry, and all the fascinating details of the chase. Old William gave him more lessons in archery, and his first instruction in the use of the sword, and riding at the quintain.

This was hard work, he soon discovered, for the sword of those days was a heavy weapon. But Peter, despite aching arm and shoulder muscles, learnt how to hold the sword, how to deliver a cut with all his weight behind it, how to guard a downward blow, and spent many hours in practice under William's critical eye.

Then he was promoted to the saddle, and shown the far more difficult business of steering a horse, and holding a shield and lance simultaneously. Not for the first time in his life, Peter wished he had an extra hand.

Once he had learnt the knack of gripping the shield and reins in the left hand, and using the right one for the lance, he was made to charge at the quintain. This was a wooden shield hanging from a pole at about the height a man would be on horse back. Peter had to trot past, and strike the centre of the quintain with the point of his lance.

Nothing could be easier, he thought, as he gripped his lance tightly, and kicked his horse into a canter. But the point of the lance began to wobble as if it were in the centre of a gale, and Peter missed the quintain by several feet. He pulled up, flushing angrily, and feeling a fool.

'Keep your eye on the shield, my lord,' William said.

'But what about the lance, William?' Peter asked. 'It wobbles like anything.'

'What did I tell you, my lord? Never heed the lance! If you watch the shield, the lance will find it. Again, my lord.'

Peter managed to hit the quintain the second time, and after he had done so four times running, he began to feel that he had mastered the art. But old William soon dashed his hopes.

'Good, my lord,' he said. 'With practice every day, you may prove a useful jouster in a few years' time.'

In a few years, Peter thought! And practice every day! But that was what he had to do every day after that, until he could canter and hit the quintain every time.

It was Lord Roger who gave him his first lesson in another subject considered essential for a member of a noble family. And that was heraldry. It was, as Peter soon learnt, an incredibly complicated business, but fortunately he was not expected to learn more than the elementary principles, so that he would be able to recognize and name correctly the best known and more important coats of arms. How else, as Lord Roger pointed out to him, could he tell friend from foe in a battle when every man's face was hidden behind a visor?

Lord Roger started him on the colours, or 'tinctures' as they were called, and Peter had to recite a list of words such as 'Azure, which is blue; gules, red; sable which is black; vert, green; and . . . and . . . ' he came to a stop.

'Purpure, which is purple,' corrected Lord Roger. 'Again, Peter,' and he took Peter through the list until he was word perfect.

After that he produced a board of wood, and with a piece of charcoal drew the various shields, and showed Peter how they were divided. Peter knitted his brows, and tried to cram the names of the six little shields into his head. He muttered the titles to himself: Pale, Fesse, Cross, Bend, Bend Sinister, Saltire, Chevron, and finally Tierce.

The cross was easy enough, and so were the bends, single lines running from the one corner of the shield to the other, with the sinister going from right to left.

When he had learnt them to the Lord Roger's satisfaction, he was shown one of the few books in the castle, a beautifully illustrated manuscript of various coats of arms, picked out in gold and silver.

Peter's eyes opened with awe as he saw the book. He had seen one like it before, in a museum, and the guide had told him that its price was almost incalculable, many thousands of pounds at least.

Roger was obviously an expert on his subject, and Peter was reminded of the vicar, as the elaborate technical terms flowed from his lips. But Peter managed to grasp some of the simpler coats of arms. He saw the proud leopards of England, the chevrons of the great house of Clare. 'Gold, three chevrons gules,' remarked Roger, as he turned the page; the red Pile of Chandos, 'Gold, a pile gules'; the lions of Percy; the leopard of Brocas; the chequers of Warrenne; and so on for the next hour, until Peter's head reeled.

But still Lord Roger recited the resounding names of the great noble families of medieval England, and the trumpet-like roll of their arms with the correct heraldic description.

'And here, Peter,' he was saying, 'the shield of Devereux. Gules, a fesse silver with three roundels silver in the chief. And here, Manners, Gold, two bars azure, and a chief gules.'

Peter scratched his head, and came to the conclusion that there was something to be said for learning French irregular verbs after all.

'We ride for Valle Crucis tomorrow,' Lord Roger said, closing the book, and dropping the priceless manuscript casually on to the stone steps on which they were sitting in the sun.

'Is Glyndwr coming with us?' Peter asked.

A shadow passed over Lord Roger's pleasant face.

'Perhaps,' he said. 'He is riding now. I shall know where this time.'

'How?' Peter sat up with a jerk.

'I have had him followed,' Lord Roger said grimly. 'He is a cleverer young sprig than I took him for if he can give the slip to John of the Falcon.'

Peter would have liked to ask more questions, but the trumpets blew for the midday meal at that moment, and Lord Roger went into the hall. Glyndwr arrived a few minutes later, and Peter watched him curiously as he slipped into his seat. There was a startling resemblance to Gwyn, even down to the freckles on his nose. If only it had been Gwyn, Peter thought, with a pang of home-sickness. And why, he wondered, did not Lord Roger insist on Glyndwr learning the duties of a page? He seemed quite satisfied with just keeping a watch on the young Welsh chief.

They set off for Valle Crucis immediately after breakfast the following morning. Glyndwr did not come with them; he pleaded sickness, and Lord Roger shrugged his shoulders when the message was brought to him. Then he beckoned to John of the Falcon, and bent down from his high saddle to whisper something in the old falconer's ear. John nodded, and glanced across the courtyard towards the tower where Glyndwr had his room.

Although Valle Crucis was no more than three hours' ride away, Lord Roger took with him ten armed men as an escort, besides Robert, and Lord Roger's own servant, Gerald. Peter blinked at the size of the escort; although Lord Roger was in riding clothes, Peter knew that his fighting armour was packed in a pannier on one of the mules.

It was all extremely puzzling. The Lord Roger expected trouble, that was clear. But from where, and why, was beyond Peter. But he soon forgot the mystery in the fascination of the ride, for he had not ridden so far from the castle since his arrival.

They took the road over the hills which Peter had seen once before, when he and Gwyn had been driven to the abbey by the vicar. But though the road ran in the same direction, there was little else that Peter could recognize. There had been few farmhouses or buildings of any kind even in the twentieth century, when England and Wales could boast of a population of nearly forty-five million. But in fourteenth-century Wales, when the whole country could barely muster six million, if that, less than the modern London, the road to Valle Crucis ran through a completely empty countryside, bare, desolate, and wildly beautiful.

The hills and mountains were the same, but the neatly hedged fields which Peter had seen on his first journey had disappeared. All that was to be seen now was a vast expanse of common, gorse, tangled undergrowth, and long stretches of forest. The road itself was a rough track of hard beaten earth, hard and dusty in the summer, and a solid mass of sticky mud in the winter. Bridges were non-existent, and they splashed over the streams at shallow fords.

For the first hour, they met no one. But shortly after they had crossed a stream, Peter heard the faint tinkle of a bell. As they reached the top of the slight hill overlooking the stream, Peter saw about fifty yards ahead, a single grey-robed figure, muffled to the eyes. One hand of the person, for Peter could not tell whether it was man or woman, was holding a small hand-bell.

The sound of the bell, and the sight of the solitary walker, had a sudden and startling effect on the other members of Peter's party. The Lord Roger muttered some inaudible words under his breath, pulled violently at the reins of his horse, and galloped violently off the road. The rest, without any hesitation, or without waiting for orders, followed him, and in a minute the whole party was cowering behind a clump of trees, well clear of the road.

Peter stared at them in amazement, but thought it best to join them, and he too, twitched his reins, and cantered off the road. There must be something very startling about this single traveller, he thought, to make a powerfully armed escort run for their lives.

He glanced at Lord Roger, whose healthy brown face had paled with sheer fright.

'God preserve us,' Lord Roger muttered. His hands flickered across his surcoat as he crossed himself devoutly. 'A leper!'

A leper! Peter stared with sudden horror at the slowly approaching figure, who by this time was nearly opposite them on the road below.

'Who is it?' he whispered.

'It is Rees Evans of Llanferon, my lord,' Robert said in low tones. His eyes were fixed rigidly on the road. 'It was two years this Easter that he caught the disease.'

The bell clanked dolefully, and the wretched man shuffled past, flinging them one look of despair as he went. There was dead silence, broken at last by one farewell tinkle of the bell, and then the pathetic figure had disappeared over the brow of the hill.

From Gerald, Lord Roger's manservant, there came a muffled sob, and Peter looked at him with surprise. The man's tough bronzed face was twisted with grief, and two tears were running down his cheeks. Lord Roger patted him on the shoulder.

'He is in God's hands, Gerald,' he said with rough sympathy.

Gerald nodded, and turned his horse away.

Robert leant across, and whispered in Peter's ear.

'That was Gerald's brother, my lord,' he said.

Peter shook his head, and sniffed in the cool fresh air, and the colour flooded back into his cheeks.

'You were slow, Peter,' Lord Roger said, as they regained the road. 'Did you not hear the bell which these poor lepers must carry to give due warning to all travellers on the road?'

Peter stammered some confused reply, his brain still numbed by the horror and tragedy of that muffled figure. He trotted the next few miles in silence, until the warm spring sun, and the beauty of the scenery blew away the feeling of something unclean which had filled his head.

They met several other travellers as they neared Valle Crucis; a Franciscan friar, with the grey habit and black of his order, and the distinctive knotted cord about his waist. He threw them a quick blessing in Latin, and was bidden by Lord Roger to spend the night at Carreg Cennen.

After that they met three wandering minstrels. They too, were told by Lord Roger to go to Carreg Cennen. Any source of entertainment was welcome in those days, and minstrels could always rely on a bed for the night.

Peter sat up expectantly as they trotted up the hill that overlooked the abbey. It was from here that the vicar had shown him his first glimpse of the great monastery, and wonderful as that sight had been, it would be surpassed by what he was going to see in a few minutes. Peter grinned. What would the old vicar have given to be in his position now?

As the thought crossed his mind, he heard the notes of a deep-toned bell.

'Valle Crucis,' Lord Roger said.

Peter clapped his heels into his horse's sides, and cantered forward eagerly. He then saw that the Valley of the Cross had not changed a great deal. The steep hills on either side were still covered with gorse and heather, and the stream still wandered lazily down the centre of the valley.

But it was the abbey that had changed. Peter could remember very vividly the mass of grey ruins; now, he saw a sprawling pile of fresh white buildings, grey slated roofs, and dominating the whole, the square tower of the abbey church. It was from there that the deep-voiced bells were ringing.

In the centre of the abbey was a large square lawn, and across it Peter could see a stream of white-clad figures, making their way to the church. Outside and in the fields were dotted other figures, busy on the work of ploughing, sowing, or weeding. Two men were sitting by the side of the stream, fishing placidly.

Lord Roger rode past Peter, who was still deep in the beauty of the scene.

'I trust that my Lord Abbot has not forgotten our arrival,' he said, breaking in abruptly on Peter's thoughts. 'Thanks be to Heaven that it is not a Friday today!'

'But why not Friday?' Peter asked in surprise.

'They eat no meat on Fridays,' Lord Roger said simply. 'Fish only on that day.'

He jerked his reins, and cantered smartly down the hill towards his midday meal.

But it was the Abbey that had changed

(See page 102)

11

The Abbey of Valle Crucis

They were met inside the great entrance gate of the abbey by the gatekeeper, and as they dismounted, two monks approached. In front was a portly old gentleman in the snowy white robes of the Cistercians, and he, as Peter learnt afterwards, was the hospitaller, responsible for the reception of the more important guests of the abbey. With him was the cellarer, in charge of the ale and wine, and what was even more important, all the food and provisions of the great building. He, too, was a stout and well-fed looking man, and Peter wondered unkindly if all Cistercians were fat. But he was to learn that the monks were a hard-working and a very devout set of men.

The hospitaller muttered a brief blessing, and smiled at Lord Roger, whom he obviously knew well.

'My Lord Abbot is at High Mass, Sir Roger,' he said. 'I will take you to his lodgings, and he will greet you before dinner.'

'Good,' Lord Roger said with satisfaction. He turned briskly to the cellarer. 'Tell me, Brother Ambrose, what have you for dinner today?'

The cellarer did not seem to think there was anything out of the ordinary in this abrupt and very pointed question, for he proceeded to run over the menu without any hesitation for Lord Roger's benefit. To Peter it sounded like the last hotel he had visited with his parents, and indeed, as they were shown to their rooms in the abbot's lodging, the impression became even stronger.

He was, in fact, not far wrong, for he discovered that the monasteries were the hotels of the Middle Ages, and they all had accommodation for visitors, carefully graded to fit the rank of their guests. Distinguished noblemen, such as the Lord Roger de Blois, were given rooms in the abbot's lodgings, whilst merchants, travelling minstrels, or just plain beggars who were never turned away, were accommodated in the ordinary guest rooms. Rich people were expected to make some present to the abbey, but there was no compulsion. Lord Roger, of course, was an honoured guest, for he was the nearest Marcher Lord and had given generous gifts of land and money to the abbey.

After they had washed and changed, they were led to the abbot's apartment on the first floor. The old abbot was seated behind a large desk, littered with papers and manuscripts. Standing behind him were two monks, both tall and thin, with the kindly peaceful faces that Peter had already noticed as being the hallmark of the monks. Shut away, as they were, from the wildness and cruelty of the outside world, filled with the threat of war, sudden death, or disease, which was rampant in the medieval world, it was hardly surprising that monks became placid and calm. Every detail of their lives, from morning to night, was planned on an elaborate scale, and for the rest of their lives they would follow that rule. They had no fears, no worries, no doubts. Their future was assured, and they knew what lay ahead.

The abbot greeted his guests with evident pleasure, and introduced Peter to the two monks.

'This, my son,' he said, 'is Brother Hugh, the prior. He stands next to me in authority here. And this is Brother Francis, the master of the novices. It is he who will teach you your letters.'

Brother Francis smiled at Peter.

'We will soon make a scholar of you, my son,' he said in a curiously deep voice.

Peter nodded politely, and murmured some reply. But he was chuckling to himself. It was quite possible that he might be able to read and write far better than this grave-faced and learned monk, and could probably dazzle him with his knowledge of geography, history, or science.

They went into dinner, out through a door into the cloisters where they paused to wash their hands. The cloisters were narrow corridors, running round the central lawn of the abbey. They were open on one side, but were warmer than Peter had thought, for the great height of the church and the other buildings sheltered them from the wind.

The monks, all in white, and with the same tonsured head, were filing into the refectory, or dining-room, after washing their hands in the stone basins in the cloisters.

Lord Roger and Peter were given seats at the High Table near the abbot and the other high officials of the monastery. The meal was served by the lay brothers, the servants of the abbey, so the prior explained to Peter.

Peter found that Brother Hugh was only too ready to answer his questions, and promised to take him round the great building after dinner. There was a reason for his kindness, which Peter could not be expected to know. For to these men, Peter was the eldest son of the Lord Roger de Blois, the heir to great estates, and, they hoped, a future benefactor and friend of the abbey, as his father was.

The dinner was a good one, and Peter enjoyed his meal, listening to the prior, and watching the monks in the refectory. The room itself was a welcome change after the castle, for here there were no narrow slit windows; a monastery need not worry about sieges. Its windows were large and beautifully designed with elaborately carved stone-work.

Back in the abbot's room, Lord Roger said goodbye to his host and made the final arrangements for Peter, who was to stay at the abbey for a short time.

'I will see you in two days, then, Peter,' he added.

Peter went down to see him off. He was not very excited at the prospect, but Robert was staying to look after him, so he would have one familiar face around him.

Lord Roger patted Peter affectionately on the shoulder.

'Goodbye, my son,' he said. 'Eat well, sleep well, and God be with you!'

Peter turned away. He had become extraordinarily fond of Lord Roger, and he disliked the thought of seeing him ride away.

'Now, my son,' said the prior. 'Shall we see the abbey?'

'Please, Brother Hugh.'

'Then we shall start with the church.'

They walked across the entrance courtyard to the great west door of the church. As Brother Hugh opened the massive door, and stood aside, Peter gasped at the beauty of what he saw before him.

The nave of the abbey church stretched ahead, with a row of thick pillars on either side to hold up the lofty roof. The bright sunlight streamed in through the stained-glass windows of deep rich colours, and threw cheerful splotches of reds, blues, and greens on to the white stone floor of the nave.

Three-quarters of the way up the nave was the screen, made of oak, which divided the public part of the church from the choir, where the monks sat for their services.

The prior led the way up the nave, and under the screen. To right and left were the north and south transepts, lighted by circular stained-glass windows of an even more glorious colour than those Peter had seen in the nave.

Brother Hugh showed Peter the choir stalls, carved into countless beautiful shapes, and the High Altar with its tall candles, and wonderful array of gold and silver plate. He smiled with pleasure as he saw the expression of awed delight on Peter's face.

'It is beautiful, is it not, my son?' he said. 'It is built to the Glory of God.'

He led Peter to the south transept, walking slowly, his sandals clicking softly on the stone floor. He pointed to a flight of stairs at the end of the transept.

'Those are the night stairs,' he said. 'They lead to the dormitory, and we use them for the midnight service of Mattins, with which we begin each day.'

'Midnight!' echoed Peter.

Brother Hugh smiled.

'You think perhaps that we lead a life of idleness, my son?' And as Peter shook his head, 'Come to the cloisters, and I will tell you what we do.'

They went out of the church through a small door that gave on to the north side of the cloisters, the warmest wing, sheltered by the towering bulk of the church.

There were rows of seats here. Some were occupied by monks, resting in the sunlight, or reading manuscripts, whilst others were bent over desks, busy with pen and brushes.

'We begin with Mattins at midnight,' Brother Hugh said. 'It is cold and dark then, so we put on our night boots, take a candle, and file down the night stairs into the church. These gowns of ours are useful, you see,' he added. 'They are good places for cold hands, these sleeves, and the cowls, when pulled over the head, keep us warm.'

Peter could well believe that it would be cold in the middle of a winter night. There was no heating in the abbey, except for the kitchens and one room called the calefactory, where the monks spent some time in winter.

He could imagine the monks winding their way down the stairs at midnight, cowled and shadowy, each of them carrying a flickering candle, and surrounded by the vast darkness of the great church, icily cold, and filled with chilly draughts.

'Do you go to bed after Mattins?' he asked.

'We have another service immediately after, called Lauds, and then we return to bed. At seven we rise for Prime, the next service, and after that the lay brothers celebrate Mass.'

'But what about breakfast?' Peter felt quite hungry at the thought of this long wait.

'After Prime. Then we go into Mass, and then into the chapter house.'

He walked down the cloisters, and showed Peter the chapter house, a circular stone-roofed building, where the monks discussed the business of the abbey.

'After Chapter,' went on Brother Hugh, 'we go to High Mass, then dinner at eleven.'

Peter nodded. That would be the time he and the Lord Roger had arrived that morning.

'And after dinner?' he asked.

'We work, my son. The Cistercians are great farmers, so we go out and attend to our crops, our cattle and sheep. We sell great quantities of wool. But of course, the older monks cannot work in the fields.'

'What do they do, then?'

Brother Hugh smiled his placid smile, and gestured with his hand along the cloisters.

'They sleep, my son,' he said. 'As you will wish to do when you reach their age, and have finished your dinner. See!'

He pointed to two old monks who were dozing peacefully against the walls of the cloister, their tonsured heads nodding gently.

'Do you farm, Brother Hugh?' Peter asked, grinning as he watched the two old men.

'Not now, my son. I attend to the business of the abbey with the abbot. We see the merchants who come to buy our wool, and I keep the accounts.'

Peter followed him again, saw the dormitory with its rows of beds and cupboards, the calefactory with the fire, and the great storehouse under the lay brothers' quarters, where the monks kept the food for the winter.

'What do you do after you have finished farming?' Peter asked.

'We go into the last service of the day, Vespers, and then to bed.'

'But that's very early, isn't it?' Peter said with surprise.

'It is eight o'clock, my son, and it is dark by then. And we go even earlier in the winter.'

Peter nodded. He was always forgetting that in those days, when there was no electric light, people made the most use of the daylight, and went to bed early.

They finished their tour at the spot where they had started, in the great courtyard just inside the main entrance gates. A long queue of people was standing patiently outside a building on the right of the gate.

'What are they waiting for?' Peter asked curiously.

A quick look of satisfaction passed across Brother Hugh's face as if this was a sight that he had wanted Peter to see.

'They are waiting to see the almoner, my son. Come, and see for yourself.'

Peter soon discovered that the people were from the villages near the abbey. They had come for medicine, treatment, and help in the way of food or money.

'We turn no one from our gates, you see,' the prior said to Peter. 'That is why we are always in need of benefactions from outside. Your noble father has made us great gifts in the past.'

Peter nodded thoughtfully. When he returned to Carreg Cennen, he would ask Roger to make another gift to Valle Crucis.

The prior said that he had his work to do, and he took Peter back to the cloisters, and handed him over to Brother Francis, who was in charge of the novices.

These were young men, wearing the white habit of the Cistercians, but not yet tonsured. They would in course of time, if approved of by the abbot, become full monks. At the moment they were holding slates and pencils, and were hard at work writing.

'Here is your new pupil, Brother Francis,' the prior said, and he smiled his farewell to Peter.

'Sit down, my son,' Brother Francis said. 'Do you know any of your letters?'

'Some of them,' Peter said modestly.

'Good.' The monk handed Peter a slate and a pencil. 'We will see what you can do then. Now write me your name.'

Peter bent over the slate, and scratched down the familiar signature, half smiling to himself.

'You are quick, my son,' observed the monk in surprise. He took the slate, and pursed his lips. 'The letters are poorly formed,' he added, 'but that is no great fault, and can soon be remedied. Yes, Peter, but . . . what is this?'

He peered at the slate, and started to spell out the letters that Peter had written so quickly.

'But you do not spell your name in this manner, my son,' he said. 'S—T—A—U—N—T—O—N.'

Peter's face crimsoned. He had been caught off his guard, and no wonder, for he must have written his signature hundreds of times.

'I'm sorry, Brother Francis,' he said hastily, and held out his hand for the slate. 'I was thinking of another name.'

'Yes, that must be it, my son. Try again.'

Thankful for the excuse being accepted so readily, Peter scratched out the name, and wrote down 'de Blois'.

'Excellent, excellent,' murmured the monk. 'Now write me some other words.' He paused for a moment, and then added: 'The son of Man.'

Peter decided to spend a little more time over these simple words, otherwise he might give the game away completely, for the real Peter de Blois was not supposed to be able to write at all, he suspected.

Brother Francis clicked his tongue over Peter's effort.

'Your spelling, my son!' he said. 'Son should be spelt SONNE, and man MANNE. Now try again.'

Peter choked, and bent his head down hastily. He was kept hard at work for the next hour, and Brother Francis appeared to be more than satisfied with his progress. More than once Peter wondered uneasily if he had shown a little too much knowledge, but the monk made no comment. Anyway, Peter reflected ruefully, his spelling was ruined for life now.

The lesson was brought to an end by the deep tones of the church bells.

'Vespers,' announced Brother Francis. He turned to one of the novices. 'Hubert, do you show the Lord Peter to a bench in the nave.'

He hurried away to join the stream of monks already making their way up the cloisters to the church. Hubert was a cheerful looking young man with a mop of dark hair which would disappear quickly when he took the full vows of the Cistercian order, and received the tonsure.

'Would you follow me, my lord?' he said, and led Peter to a bench in the nave, just facing the screen.

The great bells were still booming overhead, sending out their message to the whole valley. Peter could see the monks assembling in their places in the choir stalls, and finally they were all seated, long lines of white-robed figures, motionless and silent.

The bell fell silent. There was a pause, and from the abbot's chair came a rich deep voice, intoning a prayer in Latin. Peter watched his neighbour, Hubert, and followed his actions closely during the service, for the entire service was conducted in Latin, and was completely strange to Peter.

Peter slept well that night in his comfortable room in the abbot's lodging. But he was awakened by the tolling of a bell, and as he stared into the darkness, wondering what time it was, he guessed that the monks must be getting up for the midnight service. He imagined them filing down the night stairs from their dormitory, candle in hand, their heads cowled against the chilly draughts, sleepy and cold. He snuggled under the bedclothes, and went off to sleep again.

The next day passed in much the same way. Peter attended the services in the abbey church, and spent another three hours learning to read and write, or rather how to spell in the medieval way.

During one of the pauses in the lessons, he watched an elderly monk who was at work on a manuscript in the cloisters. He was engrossed in the painting of a large capital letter, a gigantic P. By his side were palettes of gold and silver leaf. Half an hour alone was spent on one portion of the letter, and as the monk leant back to examine his work, Peter realized why there were so few books in existence then.

'What is he writing?' he asked Brother Francis.

'A life of the blessed Saint Augustine,' the monk said. 'When it is finished, it will be placed in the library. We have a large collection already. There must be a hundred books at least,' he added with pride.

Peter did not smile, as he might have done a few days ago. He possessed in his bookcase at home, quite twice that number of books himself. But if the abbey library included a hundred manuscripts such as this one, then they could boast a collection that the greatest libraries and museums of the twentieth century would have envied.

He was due to ride back to Carreg Cennen on the following day, and Robert told him that the horse would be ready in the courtyard after breakfast. He paid his farewell visit to the old abbot, who smiled at him, intoned a blessing over his head, and then patted him affectionately on the shoulder.

The prior, Brother Hugh, came down to the courtyard to see Peter ride away. As they reached the cloisters, Peter paused for a moment, and looked across the green lawn to the towering walls of the church. He had a disturbing feeling that he might never see it again as it was now. At the back of his mind was the thought of that small brass in Llanferon Church.

'May I go into the church again, Brother Hugh?' he asked impulsively.

'Of course, my son.'

They walked through the cloisters, and into the cool depths of the great nave by a small side door. The prior stood aside, and watched Peter curiously as he stared around, and then up at the lofty roof.

Peter sighed as he turned away. He would always remember it as it was then, he felt.

Robert was waiting for him with the horses by the gateway, and Peter clambered up into his saddle. He looked down, and the prior was staring up at him, his dark piercing eyes fixed steadily on Peter's face.

'God be with you, my son,' he said slowly. He frowned suddenly, and started to speak, as if he had seen something in Peter's expression that had disturbed him.

Peter flushed, mumbled a goodbye, and twitched his reins. As he rode through the gate, he turned, and looked back. The tall figure of the prior was still standing there, his face wistful and sad. He raised his hand in an odd gesture, half farewell, half beckoning Peter back, and then walked slowly back inside the courtyard.

Robert coughed. It was high time they started their journey back to Carreg Cennen. Peter nodded and they cantered up the hill. In a few minutes the valley of Valle Crucis was out of sight. There was only the deep clamour of the bells summoning the monks to High Mass to remind Peter of the great monastery he had left behind him.

12

SIR WILLIAM DE CHAWORTH

Peter rode in silence for a mile. Then his fit of brooding vanished in the delight of riding, and the warmth of the sun. The road was quite deserted, and as far as the eye could see, there was no sign of human life. But Peter had become used by this time to the emptiness of fourteenth-century England. It was with some surprise, then, that he heard an exclamation from Robert.

'Horsemen!' he said suddenly, and pointed.

Peter followed the direction of his finger. Just emerging from a clump of trees about five hundred yards to their right was a small group of mounted men. They were riding hard for the road ahead.

'Who are they, Robert?' Peter asked. He felt vaguely uneasy, after seeing the intent and anxious glance which Robert had thrown at the group.

'Welsh, I think, my lord.'

Robert pulled up his horse, and fingered the hilt of his sword uneasily. His eyes roved around the deserted landscape. Peter heard him muttering under his breath.

'Three miles to Valle Crucis,' Peter heard him say.

'Why, is there danger?' Peter demanded.

Robert shrugged his shoulders.

'It will be safer to ride back, my lord,' he said.

Peter nodded. He threw a quick glance at the horses in front. They had reached the road now, and had swung round. In a flash they were spurring down the track towards them. There was an unpleasant air of purposeful speed about the whole business.

116

'Spur, my lord!' shouted Robert.

His horse jumped forward as he dug his spurs savagely into its flank. Peter did the same, and as they thundered down the road, Peter heard a loud shout from behind.

Something screamed past his head, and he ducked instinctively. In the turf to his right there suddenly sprouted a long arrow-shaft, quivering viciously. Down went Peter's head. His back felt a very large target, as he crouched down in his saddle, and urged on his horse to its top speed. Out of the corner of his eye, he could see Robert tugging at his sword, and Peter glanced down at the short weapon hanging from his own waist. But they would be poor weapons against that party behind. They could stand out of range, and shoot them down with ease. Not for nothing had Peter watched longbowmen practise below the castle walls. Oh, for a machine-gun, he thought, or a modern sports car. They would be safe enough then.

His horse swerved to avoid a pot-hole in the rough surface of the road, and Peter looked up. Then his heart jumped with sickening violence. For riding swiftly towards the road from a side track was another group of men. Peter could see the sun flashing on their shields and armour.

'Look, Robert!' he yelled, and pulled hard on his reins.

Robert was peering ahead. His fierce scarred face broke into a grin of delight.

'Spur, my lord!' he bellowed. 'They are friends!'

Peter bent down again in his saddle, and hurled his horse forward in one last frantic effort. He must take Robert's word for it, he thought, crouching low, his back tingling with the thought of those archers behind him. Another shaft hissed past, and bounced drunkenly as it hit the hard road.

Another frightening hiss. The head of Peter's horse went up with a jerk; its feet pawed the air in its agony.

Peter toppled sideways. A violent swerve from the horse, and he shot from the saddle.

He hit the ground with a crash that drove the wind from his body, and he rolled over gasping. His dazed brain was filled with the roar of voices, and the thud of hooves. As he half struggled to his feet, a huge black horse swept past. High up in the saddle, Peter caught a brief glimpse of a vast armour-clad figure, a green surcoat embroidered with four black martlets, and a closed visor, blank and frightening with its complete lack of any expression or life.

A loud bull-like voice was bellowing orders.

'John, to the right! Hubert, guard my left! Lances to the ready! Charge when I give the word. A Chaworth! A Chaworth! CHARGE!'

Peter rubbed his face, and blinked as the eddying dust from the rough track billowed past him. About twenty yards away was a group of horsemen, all heavily armoured, and hurtling down the road in the direction of the Welsh.

But there was no fight. The Welsh turned their horses, and rode madly for the shelter of some trees about two hundred yards away. As they reached them, they turned again, and a couple of archers leapt to the ground, and arched their great bows. The rescuers swerved aside in face of that threat, and the Welsh melted into the depths of the trees. One single arrow hissed through the air, and over the head of one of the charging men.

'You are unhurt, my lord?'

Peter turned to see Robert standing by his side, his face drawn and anxious.

'I'm all right,' Peter said quickly. 'They hit my horse, didn't they?'

Robert nodded.

'Who are those people who rescued us?' Peter asked.

'Sir William de Chaworth, my lord. We could not have found a better man!'

Peter watched the riders as they cantered back to the road, for they were making no attempt to pursue the Welsh in the woods. Sir William de Chaworth! Peter remembered what Roger had told him about the knight.

The Chaworths were one of the famous Marcher families of South Wales, and their main stronghold was the great castle of Kidwelly, down on the coast. William de Chaworth was a younger brother of the present head of the family, and lived in his own castle of Llandarn, about ten miles from Carreg Cennen. But his chief claim to fame was his reputation as a jouster. To use the language of the twentieth century, he was the unbeaten heavyweight champion of the Marches, for there was no knight west of Gloucester who could stand up to Sir William in the tournament.

He cantered up to them, and pushed up the visor of his helmet. Peter saw a brown weather-beaten face, shrewd and good humoured, with grey eyes that at the moment were filled with delight as if he had enjoyed the brief skirmish, as undoubtedly he had. He was an immense man with broad shoulders made even larger in appearance by his armour; his chest was as big as a barrel, and not even the thick plates of iron on his arms could conceal the great muscles of his forearms.

'Why, it is young Peter de Blois!' Sir William exclaimed as he saw Peter. His voice matched his appearance; it was deep and booming, and came from the depths of his mail-clad chest.

'And what are you doing so far from Carreg?' demanded Sir William. 'Your father should take greater care, with these roving Welsh about. They are restive these days.'

'I was riding back from Valle Crucis, sir.'

'At the abbey, eh?' Sir William chuckled. 'And how is that portly wine cask, the abbot?'

He roared with laughter at the sight of Peter's shocked face.

'You need not look so horrified, boy,' he said. 'The abbot is a good friend of mine, and I bear him no lack of respect. But you must admit that he does not look amiss at a good tankard of Rhenish wine, or a platter of good beef. Nor is he the thinnest of mortals! Neither am I!' And he thumped his great chest with a noise like a drum, and exploded into thunderous laughter.

'Thank you for saving us, sir,' Peter said, taking a quick liking to this cheerful Marcher Lord.

'I enjoyed it, boy,' boomed Sir William. 'Now, you had best ride with us to Llandarn, dine, and then go on with an escort to Carreg.'

Peter glanced at Robert, who nodded, and in a few minutes they were on their way, Peter riding between Sir William and his eldest son, John de Chaworth, a squire of about seventeen years of age.

They chatted about the topics with which Peter was by now becoming familiar: hunting, clothes, food, armour, and hawking. Peter received much sound advice on how to handle his goshawk, and listened eagerly to Sir William's remarks on tilting. This was a chance to pick up some useful hints from an expert.

'You are coming to the joust at Kidwelly, Peter?' John de Chaworth asked.

'I didn't know about it,' Peter confessed.

'It is in ten days' time. Your father will take you, I expect.'

'Oh, Roger is sure to be there,' Sir William chimed in. 'He never misses a joust.'

'I hope so,' Peter said. A medieval tournament was something he must not miss on any account. 'Are you going to tilt, John?'

'In the squires' class, Peter. My uncle, Gilbert de Chaworth, is giving a cup, and if I win, he will knight me.'

The rest of the conversation was entirely devoted to a discussion between father and son on such questions as the correct holding of the lance, the use of the sword, and every possible detail of tilting. The argument was only ended when they reached Llandarn.

The castle was much the same size as Carreg Cennen, and was perched up on the side of a hill, dominating the stream below, and the small straggling village that seemed to cling to the skirts of the castle as if for protection. Peter examined the scene with delight. He was still thrilled by such a sight; the stark grey walls, the thick towers at each corner, the towering gatehouse, and the pennon of the Chaworths fluttering proudly from a tall flag-pole.

Peter left Llandarn an hour later with an escort of ten men from Sir William's garrison. He was waved out of sight by Sir William himself, the Lady Margaret de Chaworth, and John, who had promised to look out for him at Kidwelly in ten days' time.

They met with no further incidents on the road. The usual travellers passed, wool merchants on their way to Valle Crucis to buy the wool for which the abbey was famous; wandering minstrels, pedlars and an occasional friar. But of Welsh bands there was no sign.

As the turrets of Carreg Cennen rose in sight over the hills, Peter wriggled with pleasure. He was by this time beginning to think of the castle as home, and he was looking forward with pleasure to seeing the familiar faces of Lord Roger, the Lady Marian, and little Henry.

They all came down to the bottom of the steps of the hall to greet him, and Peter flushed with delight at the obvious warmth of their reception. As he straightened himself up after bowing to the Lady Marian, he caught a fleeting glimpse of Glyndwr. The young Welsh chieftain was standing at the top of the stairs, and he was staring at Peter.

For a second, and no more, his face was a mask of bitter hatred and disappointment, and then, as if wiped away with a sponge, the ugly expression vanished, and he smiled in a friendly fashion. Peter frowned as he followed the others through the hall, and up the stairs into the solar. Perhaps he might have been mistaken; surely Glyndwr had nothing to do with the attack and ambush by the Welsh up in the hills?

'You had a good journey home, Peter?' the Lady Marian asked.

Peter hesitated, and glanced round the room. But Glyndwr was not there.

'We were ambushed by the Welsh,' he blurted out.

'What!' Lord Roger stepped forward quickly, his face dark with fury. 'Quick, Peter! Tell me what happened!'

He listened with rising anger to the story, but when Peter came to the arrival of William de Chaworth, Lord Roger's grim face broke into a broad grin.

'I warrant William enjoyed the fight, if fight there was,' he said, and in his enthusiasm, forgot for a moment the seriousness of the situation. 'You should see William's sword play. He has a stroke that catches you on the side of the helmet. Like this!'

He snatched up a stick, and swung it vigorously.

'He feints, and then comes straight through,' he said, and the stick whistled past Peter's head. 'And with a lance!' Lord Roger stopped, as if there were no words to describe Sir William's skill on horseback.

'But why did these Welsh attack us?' Peter asked, avoiding any further sweeps with the stick.

Lord Roger frowned, and threw the stick on to the floor.

'I see that you need a lesson in history, Peter,' he said. 'Look here!' He crossed to a chest near the wall, and pulled out a map.

Peter bent over it eagerly. It was a map of South Wales, and despite the crudeness of the drawing, compared with a modern ordnance map, the details were perfectly clear.

Lord Roger's finger traced a line along the coast.

'All the lands here,' he said, 'are held by the Marcher Lords. The de Clares have Glamorgan and Pembroke; Gower is under de Braose. The Chaworths are at Kidwelly.' And he ran through the names of the great Norman barons who had carved out estates for themselves in South Wales, and at the expense of the Welsh chieftains.

'Do the Welsh hold any land now?' Peter asked.

'Oh, yes, but further inland. Our nearest neighbours are here,' and Lord Roger's finger stabbed at the map, indicating a point quite close to Carreg Cennen. 'There at Llangaddock, is Maelgwyn, young Glyndwr's father. And there are other Welsh chiefs north of Carmarthen, and up in Cardigan.'

'Don't they ever try to get their lands back?' Peter asked.

Lord Roger laughed shortly.

'They do indeed, Peter, but they are divided. They have ever been so, and that is why we have held our own against them.'

'Have they ever attacked Carreg Cennen?' Peter remembered the care Lord Roger had taken over the state of the ditch, and the constant guards on the walls and gatehouse.

'They came here in my father's time,' Lord Roger said, pushing the map away. 'I was a boy, but I can remember it well. Rhys Ap Maredudu of Dryslwyn was the ringleader.

The king was in Gascony, so it seemed a good opportunity.'

Peter sat down, his face alight with interest.

'What happened?' he asked quickly.

'What you might expect,' Lord Roger said, and laughed. 'They besieged us, but Carreg is impregnable on three sides, and they had no trebuchets for the walls facing the valley.'

'What's a trebuchet?'

'A great sling for throwing rocks and boulders against the walls,' Lord Roger explained. 'They wasted three days sitting outside, and then marched south. Edmund of Cornwall, who was Regent for the king in his absence, raised an army from the barons, and Rhys fell back on his castle at Dryslwyn. They held out for fifteen days, and then surrendered when Edmund broke in.'

'And Rhys?'

'He escaped. But they caught him later,' Lord Roger added grimly, 'and he was hanged!'

There was a short silence, while Peter pored over the map.

'Do you think they will rise again?' he asked.

'When it suits them,' Lord Roger said, almost indifferently. 'A local rising, with Glyndwr's father at the head.'

'What!' Peter stared at him. This casual remark was staggering. But then, as he realized later, Lord Roger had spent his whole life in an outpost thrust deep into the heart of the Welsh territory, and one more rising was a mere incident to him.

'But isn't it dangerous to have Glyndwr here?' Peter said uneasily.

'On the contrary, Peter,' and Lord Roger chuckled. 'As long as he is inside the castle, Maelgwyn will make no move. It is when Glyndwr leaves that the trouble will start. So we shall have that much warning. And he is being watched closely. Why else do you think I have him here? As a page?' he laughed again.

Peter had to be content with that, and the conversation turned to the joust at Kidwelly, to which Lord Roger promised to take Peter, much to his delight.

Peter was given the job of cleaning Lord Roger's armour, and a laborious task it was. Every link of the mail had to be burnished, and the iron plates scoured until they shone like silver. The great gauntlet on his shield was repainted, his sword received a new grip, straps were mended, and all the leather-work carefully cleaned and greased.

Last task of all was the final sharpening of Lord Roger's great sword. Peter went to the castle smithy, and watched the shower of sparks as they shot off the grindstone.

'Enough, my lord?' asked the smith.

Lord Roger ran a critical finger along the razor-like edge, and nodded.

'Now the misericorde,' he said.

Peter watched the grim work on the small dagger, the misericorde, carried by all knights, and used in desperate hand-to-hand fighting if the sword were broken or lost. It could be thrust through a chink in the other man's armour.

'Do people ever get killed in jousts?' he asked, for he was under the impression that they were sporting events of the time.

'Sometimes,' Lord Roger said. 'If the lance splinters badly, there is a chance that you may get the point in the eye. I have known it happen. But that is unusual. Broken ribs or legs are the usual reward for a bad fall.'

13

KIDWELLY CASTLE

It was a large party that left for Kidwelly and the great joust. Besides Lord Roger himself, there rode the Lady Marian, Peter, Glyndwr, and their respective servants, together with a troop of archers and men at arms. Some of the former would be competing in the archery contests.

It was not a long journey to Kidwelly, and they left soon after breakfast. They struck the coast at the point where the modern town of Llanelli would one day stand, and then followed the coast road, past the sand dunes of Pembrey.

Lord Roger had told Peter that he should be able to see the walls of Kidwelly from several miles away, and Peter kept his eyes fixed on the road ahead. He knew that Kidwelly was one of the strongest castles in Wales, and he was anxious to see a great medieval fortress in all its glory.

He was not disappointed. After a few miles, he was able to pick out the grim walls of the castle, and as they rode nearer, he saw the details of the fortress. The main buildings stood on a mound overlooking the river, which was the strongest side, so the chief defences were concentrated elsewhere, where there was no natural protection. The river had been diverted to make a moat, and two lines of curtain walls had been built, one inside the other.

Dominating the whole castle was the immense gatehouse, making the Carreg gatehouse a mere dolls' house in comparison. It was quite sixty feet high, and towering above that again was a single watch tower, at least a hundred feet above the ground.

They were met inside the gatehouse by Gilbert de Chaworth, their host. He was a smaller edition of his brother, William, a red-faced and cheerful-looking man, portly of figure, and with a shining bald head that seemed as if it had been specially polished to an unusual degree of brilliance for the occasion.

He greeted Lord Roger and the Lady Marian with obvious delight as old friends, and beamed at Peter, to the accompaniment of a gigantic thump on his shoulders.

'Space is limited, Roger, I fear,' he said, as he led them to the inner ward of the castle. 'Some of the guests are sleeping in tents. I have put you in the tower next the chapel.'

Peter followed the others, through the crowded courtyard, filled with servants rushing here and there with panniers of clothes as the horses of the guests were unloaded. From the great kitchen came a tremendous blare of sound, which was hardly surprising, for Gilbert explained that there would be forty at least at the high table alone that night, and more were expected the next day.

'I have put your boy in with young John,' Gilbert said, puffing loudly as he reached the top of the winding stairs.

Peter found himself pushed into a tiny room, and there sitting on one of the truckle beds was John de Chaworth.

'Welcome, Peter,' he said, jumping to his feet. 'Is your baggage brought up yet? The trumpets will sound for dinner soon, and my Uncle Gilbert waits for no man when the first course is served.'

Peter was delighted to see John again, and they chattered incessantly as they dressed for dinner. John was full of the prospects for the squires' contest.

'Are any of the other squires good?' Peter asked.

'Two only,' John said. 'There is Henry de Braose, and
Alain de Camville of Llanstephan. I was a page with them
at Cardiff Castle, and I have ridden against them both. I
think I can beat them, though.'

'Well, I'll back you,' Peter said, as he examined his best
cote-hardie and liripipe, before following John down the
stairs, and across the inner ward to the hall.

This was a far larger building than the hall at Carreg
Cennen, and so was the solar beyond. This room was
already three-quarters full when they arrived. It was a
long apartment, with tapestried walls, and a huge fireplace,
decorated with the Chaworth martlets. A small log fire
smouldered there, for although the weather was not
particularly cold, these medieval castles, as Peter had
already discovered, were chilly places, filled with icy
draughts.

Peter found himself in the centre of a representative
gathering of South Wales Marcher Lords, and their ladies,
a brilliantly dressed and gorgeous collection of people, the
colour of whose clothes would have dazzled even the
brightest of peacocks.

The ladies' gowns were long and sweeping, their hair
was trained into many weird and wonderful fashions, and
their jewellery was a mass of shimmering stones and
bracelets.

But the men were no less magnificently arrayed, and
Peter blinked with delighted surprise as he tried to take in
the parade of gorgeous cote-hardies and family crests, all
vividly lighted by the hard glare of the torches stuck in
holders on the walls.

The noise was terrific. The men strutted and paraded,
and struck elegant attitudes in their superb clothes, whilst
the ladies swept majestically from one group to the other.
Every newcomer was greeted with a bellow of welcome
from the men, for after being isolated, as they were for so

many weeks at a time, they were delighted at the chance of meeting each other.

'And how is young Peter?' boomed a voice from just behind Peter. A fist like a ten-ton hammer caught him between the shoulders.

Peter tottered, regained his breath, and looked up. It was Sir William de Chaworth, his red face creased in a grin of welcome.

'Very well, thank you, sir,' Peter gulped, moving cautiously out of range. 'Are you jousting tomorrow, sir?'

'I am indeed, Peter. I feel in the mood to knock the stuffing out of some of these fellows,' and Sir William glanced around the room, as if he was quite prepared to take on the whole glittering collection at one go.

A harsh blare of trumpets sounded from the courtyard, and Gilbert de Chaworth marshalled his guests into the hall, and around the long tables.

Peter found himself sitting with John de Chaworth, and was introduced to some of the squires, including John's two friends and rivals, Henry de Braose, and Alain de Camville. He still found it strange to be named as Peter de Blois of Carreg Cennen.

It was, he found, a busy meal, for the squires had to wait on their lords, and a long and elaborate meal it was that Gilbert de Chaworth put before his guests.

During the intervals they discussed the chances of the tournament, at the squires' table. William de Chaworth was considered the favourite, Peter gathered, although there were several knights expected from across the Severn, and who had great reputations as jousters. Peter was filled with a glow of pride when he heard Lord Roger's name mentioned several times as a likely runner-up for the prize.

'How do they decide?' Peter asked his neighbour, Alain de Camville, a sturdy thick-set young man.

'All the knights run a certain number of courses,' Alain explained, 'or else they draw their names from a helmet. Those who win that round, ride again, until there are but two left.' It was, as Peter soon gathered, a simple knock-out contest, and would probably be followed at Kidwelly, as there were so many entries.

'They award points, you see, Peter,' Henry de Braose said. 'So many for a true hit on the shield, or more if you strike the helmet. If both knights hit, then the point goes to him who sits in his saddle without swaying back from the blow. And, of course, if you unseat your man, then you win outright.'

It all sounded dangerous to Peter, and he remembered what Lord Roger had said about the lances splintering.

'They use blunted lances,' John said, when Peter mentioned that. 'They splinter very easily, so there is no danger of their penetrating the armour. And to make certain, a knight throws his lance clear when it breaks, in case the jagged end will catch in his opponent's helmet.'

Peter was nudged by Robert, who was standing behind, and he hurried off to refill Lord Roger's tankard. He stood there for a moment, listening to the conversation between Lord Roger and Sir William, and watching with fascinated eyes the incredible scene at the high table with its fierce wild colours, the babel of conversation, and quick gestures of jewelled hands.

'Who is that sitting next to Edward Clifford of Llandovery?' Lord Roger asked.

William leant forward, and peered down the table.

'The man with the hart emblazoned on his cote-hardie?'

'Yes. It's the Fitz-Osborne badge, I believe.'

William sat back, and frowned as he picked up his tankard of wine.

'Yes, that is Fulk Fitz-Osborne,' he said. 'He rode in today from across the Severn.' Sir William turned an unusually serious face towards Lord Roger. 'He is a dangerous man, Roger,' he said in low tones. 'Watch for him, if you meet him in the lists.'

Lord Roger laughed confidently.

'I can take care of myself, William,' he said.

'None better,' Sir William said. 'But Fulk is not a fair fighter, and he treats a joust as an excuse for breaking bones. It was he who killed young Henry de Pagenel at Chepstow in the great tournament there last summer.'

Lord Roger nodded. 'I heard of that,' he said. 'But it was a fair fight, I was told.'

William shrugged his wide shoulders.

'Perhaps so. They were fighting on foot, with choice of weapons. Henry stumbled, and Fulk hit him with his mace. A fair blow, you may say, but Fulk is a powerful man. There was no need for such a blow. Henry's neck was broken.'

Lord Roger frowned, and examined Fulk's dark sulky face.

'Well, I will watch out for them, then,' he said, and held out his tankard for Peter to refill.

Dinner ended at last, and was followed by a couple of hours' entertainment, with jugglers, minstrels, and singers. The guests were full of good food and wine by this time, and the applause was long and deafening after each singer had finished. As they all filed back into the solar, Fulk's guests were in a noisy elated mood.

Peter followed close on John's heels, and near Henry de Braose. Just as he entered the room, a dog bounced against his legs, and he dodged hurriedly. He cannoned into a tall man standing in front. It was Fulk Fitz-Osborne.

Fulk whipped round with an oath, saw Peter, and cuffed him viciously across the head. Half off his balance, Peter slipped, and fell full length on the floor.

'Mind your hands, you filthy little scullion,' growled Fulk as Peter stood up, brushing his hose.

A furious and familiar voice resounded across the crowded room. It was Lord Roger.

'And you mind yours, too, Fulk!' he roared. 'That was my son!'

The two men, their faces flushed with anger and wine, glared at each other.

'Your brood, de Blois, is he?' Fulk said. 'Then teach him some manners before I take my whip to him.'

Lord Roger's face went purple. He stepped forward, and raised his hand. But it was caught by William de Chaworth, who pushed his great bulk between the two men, and Gilbert stepped hastily forward towards Fulk.

'My lords, my lords,' he said placatingly. 'Fulk, I am certain that you acted in haste when you struck Peter de Blois here.'

But Fulk was in no mood for an apology. His swarthy face and heavy dark brows scowled down at Gilbert de Chaworth.

'Teach your guests to keep their pages in order then, Gilbert!' he said.

Gilbert stepped back. His cheerful face hardened, and his voice was chilly as he spoke.

'This is my house, Fulk,' he said, 'and I permit no man to say—' But he got no further. For Lord Roger, still brimming with fury, and spoiling for a quarrel, interrupted.

'I will settle this, Gilbert,' he said. 'Tomorrow, Fulk, in the lists?'

'As you wish,' Fulk snapped. He turned his back, and stamped out of the room.

The silence was broken by the Lady Marian. She put an anxious hand on Lord Roger's sleeve.

'What have you done now, Roger?' she said like a nurse rebuking a young boy.

'Nothing, Marian,' Lord Roger said, 'I shall do that tomorrow. That foul-mouthed lump is going to have a lesson in manners that he will remember for a long time.'

A chorus of laughing encouragement went up from all the others in the room, and Gilbert de Chaworth clapped Roger on the back. It was obvious that Fitz-Osborne had few friends.

Peter wandered off to bed on a nod from the Lady Marian. But the glamour of the evening, with its wonderful pictures of medieval splendour, had gone. He was still sitting moodily on his hard truckle bed when John de Chaworth came in an hour later.

'Good heavens,' John exclaimed, when he saw Peter's face. 'What on earth is the matter, Peter?'

'The fight tomorrow, John.'

'What, between Sir Roger and Fulk Fitz-Osborne?' John pulled off his long dangling liripipe, and laughed. 'You can keep your worries for Fulk,' he said.

'But he's a dangerous fighter,' Peter said. 'I heard your father say so at dinner.'

'So he is. But Sir Roger is reckoned the best swordsman in the Marches, Peter. It is generally thought that my father has no equal in the saddle, or with the sword, except for Sir Roger. They fought last summer in the great joust at Pembroke Castle. They were exchanging blows for half an hour before the heralds separated them, and my father was glad to see the end of the fight, I can tell you.'

Peter sat up with a far more cheerful expression when he heard this. He had had no idea that Lord Roger was so fine a swordsman. If he could make the great Sir William feel glad to stop, then he must indeed be a match for anyone.

Immediately after breakfast the next day, he went to Lord Roger's room, in order to help in the lengthy business of dressing for the joust. Peter had become used to medieval clothes by this time, but he was amazed by the amount of stuff that Lord Roger wrapped around himself.

First came a shirt and drawers of thick wool, over which was pulled a thick padded garment called the haqueton. Despite the thickness and bulk of these underclothes, they were essential, if a knight's skin was not to be rubbed and chafed by the mail armour.

'Now, my hauberk,' panted Lord Roger, as he tugged on the mail trousers, and fastened them securely round his waist.

Peter staggered across the room with the hauberk, the mail shirt. With many grunts, Lord Roger pulled it over his head, and dragged it into place, until it covered his shoulders and chest, and fell as far down as his knees, tapering off to a point as Peter had noticed when rubbing the brass in Llanferon church.

'Good!' gasped Lord Roger, and collapsed with a clatter on to his bed which creaked ominously under his weight. 'The sollerets, next, Peter, and see that you buckle them tightly. I lost one in a joust last year, and nearly lost my toes as well.'

The sollerets were narrow plates of metal that were fastened over the feet.

Lord Roger twiddled his feet experimentally, and nodded his approval. 'Now the demi-jambarts,' he said.

Peter had learnt the curious half-French names of the pieces of armour now, and he brought over the long plates of iron that were strapped around the legs like cricket pads. Then came the demi-brassarts which went on the arms, and finally, the vambraces, over the forearms.

They were all heavy and cumbrous pieces of iron, and as Peter stood by to examine the result of his buckling, he wondered how Lord Roger could even raise his arm or leg, let alone swing a sword.

But there was more to come.

'My cyclas,' Lord Roger said.

This was the long flowing surcoat of silk, coloured green. It was sleeveless, and fell down to the knees behind, but in front no further than Lord Roger's waist, so that the pointed end of the hauberk could just be seen. A great silver gauntlet was embroidered on the breast.

Lord Roger buckled his long sword around his waist, and then picked up the deadly little misericorde.

'I may need this today,' he remarked. 'I think Fulk will fight à l'outrance.'

'A what?'

'A l'outrance. To the death!'

Peter gasped as he heard the significant expression.

'But will you be all right, sir?' he asked. 'It was all my fault, too.'

'You need not worry, Peter,' Lord Roger said. He laughed. 'It is Fulk who is worrying. Besides, I am wearing my new bascinet,' he added.

Now the Lord Roger's bascinet was his secret pride. As Peter had already discovered, he was always ready to try any new idea, and had actually made several alterations of his own in this particular helmet. Up to that time, knights used to wear a mailed hood over their head, known as the coif de mailles, which protected the vulnerable parts of their neck and throat. Over that again came the great helmet, a heavy and clumsy piece of iron, with eye holes.

But some enterprising knights were now changing to the bascinet, a lighter helmet, with flaps of mail hanging down over the neck, and so doing away with the coif de mailles.

Lord Roger had designed his bascinet himself, and had added a movable visor, which he could raise when not actually fighting. On the old-fashioned type, the whole helmet had to be taken off. This visor came to a sharp point, like a pig's snout, and later came to be known as the 'pig-faced bascinet'.

Lord Roger carefully slid his head inside the bascinet, adjusted the mail flaps, or 'camail' as they were called, round his neck, and beamed with delight.

'This will surprise William de Chaworth,' he said. 'He is always complaining that he can never breathe inside his helmet.'

At that moment, the visor dropped with a loud clang, and shut off the rest of his speech, which emerged as a muffled boom from within the helmet. He pushed it up quickly, and frowned.

'I must fix that more firmly,' he said.

'Why not hold it up with a small buckle?' Peter suggested, suddenly remembering a picture he had seen of helmets in one of Mr Evans's books.

'The very thing, Peter!'

The door opened, and the Lady Marian entered.

'Ha, Marian! What do you think of me?' demanded Lord Roger.

He strutted round the room, clanking and clattering like a squadron of heavy tanks. Lady Marian smiled at him affectionately, and nodded.

'Indeed, Roger,' she said, 'you look very fine.'

Peter agreed. Lord Roger did look superb. Every piece of his armour shone like silver, and the long flowing cyclas showed off his tall figure. His brown determined face peered out fiercely through the visor.

'But your helmet, Roger?' exclaimed the Lady Marian. 'Where is your tilting heaume?'

'Out of date!' exclaimed Lord Roger. 'This will set a new fashion. It's lighter, stronger, and far safer. And the visor. See!'

They did see. Clang! Down it crashed.

'May the fiend fly away with it!' muttered Lord Roger as he pushed it up again.

'But are you sure it will be safe?' asked the Lady Marian anxiously.

'Of course,' Lord Roger said confidently. He told Peter to carry his shield, and clattered down the stairs to the inner ward.

Waiting for him there was Sir William de Chaworth, fully armed, a glittering immense figure. He had not yet donned his huge tilting heaume, and his head was covered with the *coif de mailles*. Behind him was John armed from head to foot.

'Ah, there you are, Roger,' boomed William. 'I was just about to—' He broke off suddenly, and peered at Lord Roger. 'But what in the name of the saints is that on your head?'

'My new bascinet,' Lord Roger announced with pride. His hand shot up hastily, just in time to stop the visor clanging down again on his nose.

Sir William did not notice the movement. He was walking slowly round, peering at the bascinet with the greatest interest.

'I like it, Roger, I like it,' he said. 'I saw Hubert D'Abernon in one at Chepstow last summer. But you have improved on his. I must have one made immediately. You will let me copy it?'

Lord Roger beamed with delight, and thumped William on his mailed shoulder. They walked out of the gatehouse, chattering loudly, whilst the others followed.

14

The Joust at Kidwelly Castle

The lists had been set up in the meadows below the castle, and they consisted of a long, narrow stretch of turf, enclosed on each side by wooden barriers. A small stand had been erected for the more distinguished spectators and their ladies, whilst opposite that, the ground was already filled with a noisy and jostling crowd from the surrounding countryside.

At each end of the lists were tents for those taking part in the jousting, and the pennons of these knights fluttered above, a mass of cheerful colour. Peter was able to pick out most of those belonging to the Marcher Lords; the lions of Camville of Llanstephan, the wedges of Braose, the bend and lion of Bohun of Brecknock, and with a thrill of pride, he saw the familiar Gauntlet of de Blois.

There were others new to him, and John de Chaworth explained that they belonged to knights from beyond the Marches, such as the eagle of Monthermer, the gold bars of Harcourt, and the hart of Fitz-Osborne.

Over the stand itself there waved two pennons: the black martlets of Gilbert de Chaworth, and by its side the most famous coat of arms in the Marches, the three gold chevrons of the great Clare family, renowned throughout England and Europe, the Earls of Gloucester, and Lords of Glamorgan, with castles and lands scattered all over the country.

The draw for the jousting was made by Gilbert de Chaworth. Names had been scratched on pieces of wood, and were then drawn from a helmet. Lord Roger and

Fulk, who were to settle their quarrel, were not drawn; they would oppose each other in any case.

Gilbert announced the conditions of the joust.

'A single course with blunt lances, my lords,' he said. 'If there is no decision, the heralds will order another course.'

There was a snort of disgust from Fulk Fitz-Osborne.

'For my part,' he said in his rasping voice, 'I would wish to carry my argument with de Blois further than a mere breaking of blunt lances.'

'By all means,' Lord Roger said eagerly. 'Pointed lances, and *à l'outrance.*'

'No, no,' protested Gilbert de Chaworth.

'You are feeling squeamish today, de Chaworth,' Fulk sneered.

Gilbert flushed, then checked the hasty motion of his hand.

'As you wish, Fulk,' he said. 'And if you are still in the mood for some exercise after Sir Roger has finished, then I shall be pleased to run a course with you.' He turned his back on Fulk, and walked away.

At that moment the trumpets sounded, and the lists were cleared for the first course of the day. This was to be between Sir William and one of the Bohuns.

Peter watched with interest as Sir William prepared himself for the course. The veteran and experienced jouster took his time. He chose a lance with the utmost care, discarded two that John handed to him, felt their balance carefully, then satisfied, drew on his great tilting heaume, thrust his hands into heavy iron gauntlets, and was pushed up into the high saddle of his horse.

He tucked the butt of the lance under his armpit, and twined his fingers lovingly round the polished grip. His shield slid over his left arm, and the reins were gripped tightly by his left fist. As the trumpets blared harshly, he clapped his spurs into his horse's sides, and trotted to the end of the lists. To Peter, and to many of the onlookers, he was a vast and impressive figure, as solid as the Rock of Gibraltar. How could anyone stand up to that tremendous combination of weight, skill and experience?

From the side of the lists came the stentorian bellow of the herald, a gorgeously arrayed figure, and the chief umpire and referee of the whole proceedings.

'My lords and ladies,' he shouted. 'A course with lances between Sir William de Chaworth of Llandarn, and Sir Ralph Bohun of Brecknock.'

The excited murmur of the crowd died away into an expectant hush. Both jousters were well known, and Sir William was, of course, the acknowledged champion of the Marches. That Kidwelly crowd, on the lovely spring morning in the fourteenth century was just as anxious to see its favourite perform as any modern crowd at a Test Match waiting for its hero to go into bat.

The trumpets blared for the last time, and the herald's wand flashed down. From the crowd came a long-drawn 'Aaaah!' and then silence.

It was broken by the loud drumming of hooves, as the two huge horses trotted towards each other, working up to their full speed. Their riders were crouched low in the saddle, only the tops of their helmets showing above the gaily-painted shields. They were two great machines, thought Peter, clenching his fists in his excitement. For there was no sign of any expression; the two great tilting heaumes were blank faces of iron.

Faster grew the pace, and with a sharp crack of splintering lances, and a loud bellow from the crowd, they struck home. Bohun struck Sir William full on the shield, but that great rider never moved in his saddle. The tip of his spear, as steady as a rock, caught the top of Sir Ralph's helmet, a shrewd and deadly blow. Bohun swayed back in his saddle, and toppled headlong over his horse's

The tip of his spear . . . caught the top of Sir Ralph's helmet

rump, hitting the ground with a clang of iron that echoed round the lists.

Peter gulped. Surely the man must be killed after that appalling smash? But already he was struggling to his feet, and then walked slowly back to his tent. Sir William pulled off his helmet, and beamed from a streaming red face at the wildly cheering crowd.

'No bones broken, Ralph?' he shouted to his unfortunate opponent.

'None, William!' Bohun waved good-humouredly to his victor, and shook his head ruefully at his downfall.

Two more courses were run after that. In neither case was there a fall, but the heralds gave the victory to the knights who had made the squarest hit on the other's shield. Only the most skilled of jousters, as John whispered to Peter, aimed at the helmet. It was extremely difficult to hit such a small target, but on the other hand, was a certain winner, if it came off.

'Now, Roger, your turn,' William said. 'Are you still set on using pointed lances?'

Lord Roger nodded, and pulled on his new bascinet.

'I mean to settle this matter,' he said shortly.

'Good!' grunted Sir William. 'Now, listen, Roger. Aim for his shield. He is no great horseman, and you may knock him off. But he is a good hand with the sword, so watch for yourself. And I hope you break his cursed neck,' he added hopefully.

'Good luck, sir,' Peter muttered, looking up anxiously at Lord Roger's determined face.

Lord Roger smiled briefly at him, and then pulled down the visor of his helmet. As the trumpets sounded, he cantered slowly to his end of the lists.

The herald raised his wand for silence.

'A fight *à l'outrance*,' he shouted, and paused as the crowd broke into an excited buzz of conversation.

'Between Sir Roger de Blois of Carreg Cennen, and Sir
Fulk Fitz-Osborne of Ludlow. These two noble knights
will run a course with pointed lances, and if there be no
decision, will continue on foot with swords.'

He stepped back, and waved his hand to the trumpeters.
The crowd, after that first outburst of excitement, were
deadly still now. A fight à l'outrance was not a common
sight. To the majority of the spectators the finer points of
jousting, the handling of the spear, and the skilful
combination of horse, shield and lance, were a mystery,
but they could all appreciate a violent fight, blood, broken
bones, a good fall, and they sensed that this would come
now. For this contest would end only when one of the two
knights was dead or unconscious.

Peter wished that he could share their delight. He felt
sick with fright. For the Lord Roger he had developed a
great affection, and this wretched quarrel, he felt, was
partly his own fault.

Both knights were rigid, waiting for the signal. Fulk was
an impressive and menacing sight, his scowling face
hidden behind his ponderous helmet. But Lord Roger
was no less imposing, and the snout-like shape of his new
bascinet gave him a fierce and ruthless appearance.

Down came the herald's wand, and the trumpets blared
their raucous spine-chilling call. Down came the lances to
the charge, and the two men pounded over the soft turf,
the hooves of their chargers throwing up big clods of
grass. The sun flashed in hard gleams on the tips of the
highly polished helmets, and Peter saw with fascinated
eyes such tiny details as Lord Roger's cyclas streaming out
in graceful folds behind him, as he crouched low, his lance,
with its deadly steel-tipped point, rigid and still, thrusting
out far ahead, aimed unerringly at his opponent.

They met with a crash, and a crack of lances. Fulk's
spear, well aimed, hit Roger's shield, and then splintered,

the broken point rising far into the air. But Roger held his seat, his knees clamped like iron to his horse's side. He too, hit Fulk, fair and square on the shield, with all his weight behind the blow.

Fulk swayed, recovered his balance, and galloped past to the end of the list, while the crowd roared its appreciation. There was little doubt about their favourite. Roger was a local Marcher Lord, whilst Fulk came from the borders. A roar of 'de Blois! de Blois!' went up from all sides.

'This new bascinet is a marvel,' Lord Roger said, as he dismounted, and handed over his horse.

'We shall see if it stands a sword blow,' William said.

'Of course it will,' Lord Roger snorted, and strode off, clanking loudly at every step, to where Fulk was waiting for him in the centre of the lists. The long broad-bladed swords flashed in the sun as they stood there, whilst the herald gave the signal.

Peter clenched and unclenched his hands. He felt that he could not bear to look. For this was no longer a game. If Fulk had his way, he would have no compunction in smashing in Lord Roger's brains, and the man looked horribly dangerous, as he swung his sword idly, and with accustomed ease.

The herald raised his hand, and Fulk stepped forward. With the same quick movement he smashed it down at Lord Roger's head.

Peter gasped, and shut his eyes. But he need not have worried. Roger moved his shield, and guarded the vicious blow. As he did so, he thrust hard at Fulk's throat, at the spot where the camail covered the vulnerable spot over the windpipe.

Then with a clatter, they set to in earnest, hammering furiously at each other, bending, ducking, jumping back, raising shields to guard against sudden strokes, the blades of their swords flashing in and out with sharp flickers of light as the sun caught the polished surfaces.

From Sir William came a running commentary of advice, prayers, and grunts of satisfaction or dismay.

'Good, Roger! Now, the point! So! Up! Up! Quick, for your life! Oh, bravely done!'

To Peter, it was a long drawn-out agony of hopes and fears. At each furious cut from Fulk, he shivered, and clenched his hands convulsively, sometimes even shutting his eyes altogether, expecting to see Lord Roger sprawling helpless on the ground the next moment.

But Lord Roger was quite capable of taking care of himself. After a few minutes fighting, even Peter could see that Fulk was the weaker swordsman. He could not deliver such a ferocious series of cuts and thrusts as Roger was giving him at such a bewildering pace.

Fulk must have realized the position. At the speed with which they were fighting, neither man could hope to remain fresh, and then Lord Roger with his superior skill would have Fulk at his mercy. So Fulk decided to make use of his extra inch of height and reach while he was still fresh.

Gathering all his strength together, he hurled himself at Lord Roger, raining in a succession of desperate slashes, hoping to break through by sheer fury and weight.

Peter shook with fear as those tremendous blows whistled down. But Roger guarded them with calm efficiency, either stepping back quickly to avoid the heaviest, or parrying the others with sword or shield.

One more terrific cut. Lord Roger side-stepped neatly, and the blow whizzed past. But his foot slipped on a greasy patch of turf. He hesitated, swayed, and then was off his balance.

With a shout, Fulk jumped forward. Up went his arm, and as Lord Roger struggled to regain his balance, Fulk hit him a terrific blow that went past Roger's guard, and caught him full on the top of his bascinet. With a clang that resounded throughout the lists, Roger staggered back. From the crowd came a roar. They smelt blood.

Fulk leapt forward to deliver the final blow. Lord Roger was half dazed by the blow. His shield had fallen, and he was kneeling, one hand on the ground, as Fulk's next stroke came whistling down at his unprotected head.

'Up! Up!' bellowed Sir William.

Lord Roger squirmed miraculously to one side. Even so, the sword-stroke caught him on the side of his bascinet. But it was here that he was saved. For the sharp curve of the helmet caused Fulk's sword to slither off.

With a bellow, Lord Roger jumped to his feet, and put both hands to his sword. There was no time to pick up his shield. He jumped forward.

'In! In! de Blois!' yelled the crowd.

But Lord Roger needed no encouragement. He swung neatly to one side as Fulk slashed desperately at him. Then he was within the other's guard, and up went his sword. It came down with all the weight and force of his two muscular arms. With a crash, it landed on Fulk's helmet.

Fulk staggered, his arm dropped, and for a second, he stood defenceless. In a flash, Roger swung at him again, a terrific blow on the side of the helmet, and as Fulk went down, he aimed a vicious thrust, straight at the throat. With a bull-like bellow, Sir William rushed forward as the heralds stepped between the two men. Fulk was lying motionless on the turf, arms out-flung. From the stand came a roar of voices, the fluttering of scarves, and from the crowd a thunderous tumult of deafening applause.

Lord Roger pushed up his visor as William and Peter reached him. His face was streaming with perspiration, and over one eye was a dark bruise.

But he grinned broadly at them. 'And what do you think of my new bascinet now, William?' he said triumphantly.

'I must have one!' William cried. 'I will have a dozen of them!'

A group of men had gathered round Fulk. He still had not moved, and Gilbert de Chaworth pulled off his helmet.

'Well, he's still alive, Roger,' he said with a note of disappointment in his voice.

'You didn't hit hard enough,' grumbled William. 'But it will be a long time before he jousts again.'

Peter wiped his face, and walked slowly back to the end of the lists with Lord Roger. Perhaps he could enjoy the rest of the tournament now, he thought.

It was a warm and sunny afternoon, and as Lord Roger announced his intention of taking no further part in the jousting, he and Peter spent their time encouraging the Chaworth family. Sir William won his next two rounds with ease, and to his father's immense delight, John beat both his first two opponents in the squires' contest.

Peter was enjoying himself now. For it was a glorious sight, and one that he never forgot. There were so many vivid splashes of real beauty around him, that he found it difficult to decide which he liked most. Sometimes it was the horses, and their grim armoured riders; now the gay shields and fluttering pennons; the colour and pageantry of the lords and ladies in the stand; the crowded barriers with their noisy shouting spectators; the soft green of the turf; the dazzling white of the tents; the sheen of the armour, or the blue of the sky, and the slowly drifting clouds. It all blended into one perfect picture, with a background of the great castle, the long grey walls, the great towers, and the massive gatehouse.

As he tried to take it all in, he felt an urgent hand on his arm. He looked round. It was Robert, his face worried and tense.

'Quick!' he whispered. 'Where is the Lord Roger?'

Peter glanced around. Lord Roger was standing by Sir William and Gilbert de Chaworth; he caught Peter's anxious glance, and stiffened as he saw Robert. He seemed not unduly surprised, as he strode towards them; as if he were expecting trouble, Peter thought.

'What is it, Robert?' he snapped.

'The Lord Glyndwr,' Robert said. 'He has gone!'

'When? And in what direction?'

'Towards the mountains, my lord.'

Lord Roger frowned, and rubbed his chin. Gilbert and William had come up.

'What is it, Roger?'

He told them quickly, and they too frowned.

'What do you think, Gilbert?' Lord Roger asked. 'I must ride for Carreg at once. It may be a false alarm.'

'Perhaps,' Gilbert said. 'But take no chances. I was riding for Pembroke after the jousting was finished. I will wait here for news; it will be safer, if the Welsh are up.'

In a few minutes these experienced men had decided on their plan of action. Lord Roger was to ride for Carreg at once, and the Lady Marian would follow the next morning. The other neighbouring barons would return to their respective castles, and stand by for further news. Once it was known where the Welsh were concentrating, the Marcher Lords would collect, and overwhelm the Welsh with superior numbers.

An hour later, Lord Roger was riding to Carreg, with Peter by his side, and a small escort of men. They travelled as if the Devil himself were on their heels.

15

THE SIEGE OF CARREG CENNEN CASTLE

They reached Carreg Cennen long after dusk. For Peter, the last half of that ride was a nightmare. The heavy clinging darkness of the medieval countryside at night was something new to him. They rode without any lights, and if the horses had not picked their own way along the rough road, it was doubtful if they would ever have reached the castle.

But at last they saw its towering bulk loom up against the darkness. From the gatehouse came a flicker of torchlight, and as they rode up to the ditch, a loud bellow came from within.

'Halt!'

'They keep good watch,' Lord Roger muttered with satisfaction.

A figure appeared on the other side of the ditch, holding up a spluttering torch.

'It is the Lord Roger,' Robert shouted into the darkness.

'Give the password, then, and let us hear his voice.'

Lord Roger cupped his hands.

'Longbow!' he yelled, giving the word. 'Is that you, William?'

'Yes, my lord. I will lower the bridge.'

A loud creaking showed that the bridge was being lowered across the ditch. It fell into place with a thud, and they cantered across. As Lord Roger dismounted, old William came up to him, his face sharp and drawn in the red glare of the torchlight.

'We had not expected you tonight, my lord,' he said.

149

'No. I rode in haste. You keep good guard, William. We may be glad of it, soon.'

'Aha!' William chuckled with glee at the thought of a fight. 'Is it the Welsh?'

Lord Roger nodded, and issued a stream of orders, posting double sentries, and instructions for the whole garrison to stand to at dawn. Then he went to bed, and Peter did the same.

He was not awakened by any alarm that night, and when he peered through his narrow window at dawn, there was no sign of any Welsh troops outside the walls. Perhaps it was a false alarm, after all.

But Lord Roger was taking no chances. Immediately after breakfast, he sent out a patrol with the double duty of meeting the Lady Marian, and escorting her home, and at the same time to report on any suspicious move by Welsh troops. The village was warned to be ready at half an hour's notice, to bring all their cattle and stock inside the castle, and to leave as little as possible for the Welsh to plunder if they did come.

By midday, the preparations were complete. Lady Marian had arrived from Kidwelly, and the patrol had reported no sign of any hostile Welsh. But the surrounding countryside was suspiciously empty, and Lord Roger decided to bring all the villagers inside.

An hour later, and the great inner courtyard was filled with a jostling mass of villagers, cows, sheep, and animals of all kinds. The noise, the crowd, and the smells were worse than anything that Peter had experienced so far, and he had found the fourteenth century an evil smelling world at the best of times.

Nothing happened that day, nor during the night. Peter found the castle unbearably crowded and unpleasant, and he wandered out through the gatehouse, with urgent orders from old William not to go any further than the garden beyond.

It was not a large garden, and was used mainly by the Lady Marian for growing her herbs, and for the few flowers cultivated in those days. Peter found a comfortable spot near the edge of the great precipice, and wedged himself against a huge rock, and dozed in the sun.

He was feeling oddly restless; a sensation of unease had swept over him several times during the last two days, and for the first time for a few weeks, he had found himself watching the people around him with the detached eye of an observer from another age again, as he had done when he had first arrived in this strange world. As he dozed in the sun, he wondered uneasily if this was the end of his adventure. It was not the thought that it might be the end which worried him so much; it was the way in which it might end. If he knew that, he would have felt easier in his mind.

His head drooped; he had not slept well the previous night. Then, as from a great distance, he heard a dull low-pitched roaring sound. It changed to a deep drone, and he sat up quickly. As he did so, the noise died away.

Sounded like an aeroplane, he thought, and then laughed. There were no aeroplanes in the fourteenth century. Restless again, he jumped to his feet, and peered over the precipice to the awful drop down the sheer side of the cliff. Something was going to happen to him, he thought. And if he did find himself back in the twentieth century again, would anybody believe him?

The vicar would talk wisely about dreams; Gwyn would laugh and tap his head significantly. Mr Evans would worry, and ring up the doctor.

'But it isn't a dream!' Peter muttered to himself. 'I must give them some proof!'

But what proof could he give them? Was there anything he could take back with him? He gazed around, and his eyes fell to his belt. The misericorde! That would convince them. But how to take it?

Then the solution flashed across his brain. Bury it somewhere. How could anyone know that a fourteenth-century dagger was buried in a certain spot? And he could mark it with his initials!

Peter tugged at his belt and pulled out the graceful yet deadly little weapon. With the point of a sharp stone he scratched a rough P.S. on the blade, and scored it deep. Then he dug a hole with the sharp blade, and pushed the dagger in the soft earth, patting the soil back into place. Behind the hiding place was a massive outcrop of rock. That would not change much in six hundred years, he thought, and would mark the spot.

He chuckled and stood up. Then from the high tower by the gatehouse there came a loud raucous shout. The trumpets blared harshly. From within the courtyard the villagers broke into a babel of shouts. Orders were bellowed from the walls, and the whole great castle buzzed with alarm.

Peter turned, and rushed for the gatehouse.

Inside was confusion, or so it seemed, but everyone knew his post, thanks to the careful plans made by Lord Roger. Peter dashed up the stairs to the walls, and joined Lord Roger and William who were peering into the sun across the mountains.

'Is it the Welsh?' asked Peter, panting after his rush up the steep stairs.

Lord Roger nodded. He seemed remarkably calm about it, Peter thought, but he followed the direction of William's gnarled finger, as it pointed towards a gap in the hills where the road from the north came down to the valley.

Peter shaded his eyes against the strong sun. For a moment he could see nothing but a cloud of white dust rising slowly into the still air. Then some metal object flashed in the sun; then a quick succession of bright momentary gleams, brief twinkling specks through the dust cloud, and as if blurred by the distance, a vague impression of a moving mass. He had never seen such a sight before. But he could recognize it for what it was: a large body of men on the march, heavily armoured.

Lord Roger and William quietly discussed the question of raising the drawbridge, and any last-minute precautions. Then Lord Roger bade Peter help him into his armour, and they went down to the solar.

Peter himself had been fitted with a mail shirt by this time, but this was the first time he had occasion to wear it. It was heavy and cumbrous, particularly the small helmet, which was shaped in imitation of Lord Roger's famous bascinet.

It was not until an hour later that the Welsh troops came close enough to be seen in detail. They swung down into a fold of the ground, and for a time there was nothing to be seen but the tell-tale cloud of dust to show that they were still on the move.

Even Lord Roger showed signs of impatience, whilst all those on the walls waited for the attackers to reappear.

'There!' William shouted suddenly.

Lord Roger sprang to the wall, staring through the visor of his helmet. Over the brow of the hill about three hundred yards away, a group of horsemen had jumped into view.

They pulled up, and waited for a long procession of footmen to march past. Peter could see the longbows sticking up over their shoulders. The Welsh had few cavalry, that was clear, and the majority were wearing thick leather coats, topped by steel helmets.

'How many, William?' snapped Roger.

'About a thousand, my lord.'

Roger nodded his agreement. Peter felt relieved. Used to the gigantic forces of the twentieth century, numbered in their hundreds of thousands, this was a mere flea-bite. But even so, it was a large number compared to the garrison of Carreg Cennen. They had about two hundred men, counting the villagers.

'Will they attack us at once?' he asked.

'They will be bigger fools than I take them for if they do,' Lord Roger said. 'Their best chance is surprise, and they have lost that. They will come and parley, and try to frighten us into surrender.'

He was right. After some delay, four horsemen broke away from the main body, and galloped up to the gatehouse. One man was carrying a white pennon.

'Give orders to hold the fire, William,' Lord Roger said. He leant over the parapet, and grunted angrily. 'As I thought. Maelgwyn!'

'And there's Glyndwr!' Peter exclaimed.

'The filthy little traitor,' growled Lord Roger. 'If I but lay my hands on him, he will regret that he ever abused my hospitality.'

Maelgwyn was a short, stockily-built man, in mail armour from head to foot; his face was swarthy, and his voice, when he spoke, shrill and high pitched.

'I would have word with Sir Roger de Blois,' he yelled.

Lord Roger moved forward, until those below could see the great silver Gauntlet on his shield.

'I am here,' he said. 'And with more reason than you, Maelgwyn. What are you doing abroad with such a body of men?'

'I have come to regain the lands that are mine by right!' shouted the Welsh chieftain.

Lord Roger shrugged his shoulders impatiently.

'You are a hundred years too late,' he said. 'Go home in peace to Llangaddock. Else I name you as an enemy of the king.'

Maelgwyn twitched the reins of his horse in his rising anger.

'I do not recognize your king,' he said. 'We have had enough of you Norman barons. This is Welsh land.'

'I have warned you, Maelgwyn,' Lord Roger retorted. 'Remember the fate of Rhys.'

'I demand the surrender of this castle,' shouted Maelgwyn.

'You rave,' Lord Roger said contemptuously. 'If you are not out of bowshot by the time I count ten, I order my men to draw upon you.'

Maelgwyn shook his mailed fist at the faces above him on the lofty wall.

'You have asked for blood, de Blois,' he bellowed, 'and by the saints, you shall have it! When I have taken the castle, I will hang you on that flagpole, and your son with you.'

He turned his horse, and the party galloped away.

'The ranting fool,' growled Lord Roger. Old William laughed contemptuously.

Peter wished he could laugh too. But that reference to the flagpole was not a pleasant one. He glanced at it, and one hand fingered his throat nervously. But he gradually forgot his fears in the interest of watching the besiegers, and listening to the conversation of Roger and William.

He had picked up quite a good deal on the subject of sieges, for it had been part of his military education with William and he knew that the enemy were faced now with several alternative plans. The first and obvious one was to surround the castle, and starve it out. But that was a long drawn-out affair. (One great castle in Normandy had been known to hold out for six months, and the Welsh could not possibly afford to waste so much time.) They would lay themselves open to an overwhelming counter-attack from the Marcher Lords long before Carreg Cennen had reached the last of its provisions.

The second possibility was a direct attack. They could stage a surprise night onslaught, using scaling ladders, or huge movable towers on wheels, which were rolled alongside the walls, and from the tops of which the attackers could jump on to the battlements. To do that, of course, they must fill up the ditch beforehand, and that would take time.

If that failed, they could make a breach in the walls, by mining. To do this a tunnel would be dug under the walls, the foundations removed, and down would come the tower, or a section of the walls. It was the method of attack most feared in medieval days.

Another alternative, and the most successful, was to batter at the walls and the interior of the castle with enormous slinging machines called trebuchets, or smaller ones known as mangonels. When the wall started to crumble, a rush was made for the gap. The ditch would automatically be filled by the rubble from the destruction of the wall as the masonry rolled downwards.

In the opinion of those inside Carreg Cennen, any of these plans were extremely unlikely to succeed. The castle was well stocked with food, and had a permanent water supply from the well cut in the solid rock. Mining was almost impossible, for the castle was built on solid rock. A night attack, they thought, was the most likely plan, and owing to the precipice, that could be made against one side of the castle only. The defenders, therefore, would not be taken by surprise, and could concentrate all their attention on that section.

Trebuchets were the most dreaded weapon, but they were huge and cumbersome machines, and took some considerable time to make. Only well-equipped armies carried them, and the Welsh had never used them, so Peter had been told.

The Welsh, meanwhile, had spread out over the meadows below the castle. Some of them were engaged in digging furiously, and throwing up a long rampart of earth. They were just within bow-shot range, and Lord Roger ordered his men to open fire. As he did so, great clouds of black smoke began to roll up the valley from the direction of the village. The Welsh had fired the huts of the villeins. Lord Roger smashed his mailed fist down on the stone parapet, and muttered savage threats of what he would do to Maelgwyn if he could reach him.

Peter's attention was caught by some Welsh archers who were taking up their position in front of the rampart. It was clear that they were attempting to protect the men digging by giving a covering fire on to the castle walls. But surely they could not reach the top of the walls from there, Peter thought.

One of the archers pulled back, and let go. Peter watched him with idle interest. Then a rough hand hit his back, and he was crushed to the ground. He started to protest, when something whizzed over his head. From their right came a loud howl.

'Who's that?' asked Lord Roger sharply. He was on one knee behind the parapet.

'Richard, my lord. A shaft through his arm.'

Peter peered cautiously through a slit. He had a new respect for longbowmen now. The men on the walls were returning the fire. Near him was young Evan Ap Rees, whom he had often watched at the butts. He jumped to his feet, and drew back his great bow in the same motion. The shaft whistled off, and Peter watched it curve through the air, and then drop towards the line of Welsh archers. It seemed to leap at one man, and go over him. But he fell like a log, and Evan chuckled grimly as he crouched down again.

The long-range fight continued for some time, with a few casualties on each side. Meanwhile, the digging went on rapidly, and Lord Roger wondered loudly why the Welsh were making such a rampart. Some sort of shelter, behind which they could mass for a rush at the walls was quite usual, but this, as he said, was—

'Look, my lord, look!' exclaimed William. He caught Lord Roger by the arm, and pointed excitedly. Peter had never seen him display such emotion before.

A long team of horses had just come in sight over the ridge. They were tugging a high unwieldy-looking structure of wood.

'By the saints!' muttered Lord Roger. 'A trebuchet!'

In grim silence they watched while the horses pulled three of the deadly siege weapons into place behind the ramparts of earth.

Lord Roger tugged irritably at his chin, and scowled at the sight.

'They must have spent the whole winter making them,' he growled. 'Never have I seen the Welsh with such artillery before!'

Peter watched the clumsy machines as they were made ready for action. Their method of working was simple enough. There were two upright poles, nearly twenty feet high, and pivoting between these another pole, weighted at one end with a huge box filled with earth. At the other end of the pole was the sling-bag itself, in which large rocks could be placed.

As Peter watched, the pivoting pole was being dragged down against the weight of the great box. A huge rock was then placed in the sling, and let go. In a flash the tremendous weight of the box flashed down, and round swung the pole in a huge arc. As it reached the top of its swing, the rock flew out of the sling-bag, and curved up gracefully into the air.

It would never reach them, Peter thought, with amused contempt. What a fuss these people made about trebuchets! They could make no impression on those tremendous walls. But he was soon to learn his mistake.

The great rock curved up into the air still more, and passed over their heads on the left.

'Down on your lives!' roared Lord Roger, and once more crushed Peter to the ground.

He was just in time. Down came the rock at a terrific speed, and hit the stone flags of the inner courtyard with the force and noise of a bomb. It splintered like shrapnel into a hundred whizzing fragments, spraying the whole area with those deadly missiles.

From below came a chorus of shouts and screams, and the frantic noise from frightened and wounded animals. Peter gasped, and wiped his streaming forehead. He had a new respect now for trebuchets, as well as for archers.

One of the garrison rushed up to Lord Roger.

'Two men killed, my lord, and several sheep.'

Lord Roger nodded gloomily, and gave orders for all those in the courtyard to take shelter, if they could. But another stone from one of the other trebuchets whistled overhead as he spoke. That, too, hit the courtyard, and once more the fragments bounced and ricocheted all over the area. Fortunately the next few shots were not so accurate. The boulders either hit the walls, or went clean over, and disappeared over the precipice on the other side.

But the fire was kept up for an hour, until the attackers exhausted their first stock of ammunition. The archers from the walls had kept up a hot fire, too, and had slowed up the trebuchets. But the damage done inside the castle was serious enough; ten men had been killed or seriously injured, and several valuable animals had been killed.

Then the Welsh produced a fresh surprise. They wheeled into place a line of much smaller machines, mangonels, as Peter heard them called. These were worked like a huge bow, and fired rocks against the walls. They were much more accurate than the trebuchets, but fired a smaller rock, and with a shorter range. But they were useful for battering at a definite spot on the wall, and making a breach.

Fortunately for the defenders, the light began to fail, and the fire stopped. Lord Roger, who was looking worried, made his plans for the night, and sent Peter off to bed.

Peter went down to the hall for some supper. He found the Lady Marian there, quite amazingly calm. But she had been brought up in the Marches of Wales, and one more siege was merely an incident to her. The Welsh had never succeeded in capturing a single castle, and the news that they had proper artillery this time did not upset her in the least.

He swallowed some cold food, and stumbled off to bed. He was aching with fatigue, and was asleep within a few minutes.

16

Down the Precipice

Peter flung on his armour, and rushed out after Robert. He made for the walls, tugging feverishly at his sword. Here was the chance to see if old William's lessons had been useful.

The scene which met his eyes was a fantastic one: it might have been a picture of an inferno. The night was particularly dark, for the moon had not yet come up, but many torches threw a wild and flickering glare over part of the scene. There were torches on the walls, and more down below in the ditch, like a line of fireflies. From the parapet, the garrison were firing furiously over the walls. Some were hurtling down rocks, and others dropping torches to give the archers a better target.

Peter peered cautiously over the parapet, for the Welsh were returning the fire, and arrows were whistling up out of the darkness, and hissing viciously past. The ditch was filled with a seething mass of half-seen figures like an overturned ants' nest. They were working feverishly, throwing rocks and earth into the ditch to enable more of the attackers to get closer to the walls.

Over the whole nightmarish scene there rose the roar of voices, the crash of rocks being hurled down, the orders of the leaders, and the wild screams of the wounded. An occasional terrifying crash from the courtyard showed that the trebuchets were firing blindly into the darkness, and making good practice.

Shouts and brisk orders came from Peter's left. He turned, and saw the top of a ladder appear as if by magic over the parapet. A black figure leapt down, followed immediately by another. A wild hand-to-hand fight broke out, with the clash of swords on mail, and the fierce shouts from one side or the other.

Then the top of the ladder was cleared, and Peter saw a gigantic figure in full armour lean over. It was Lord Roger. He put his hands on the ladder, and then jumped back as another Welshman leapt upwards at him. Lord Roger swept back his hand, and Peter saw the great swing of his sword.

The Welshman put up his sword to guard the blow, but he was handicapped by his stance on the ladder. With a clang that penetrated even through that inferno of noise Lord Roger's sword crashed home. The Welshman swayed back, flung up his hands, and with a ghastly shriek, high pitched and agonized, disappeared from view. Peter had a brief and horrible glimpse of a sprawling figure falling limply into the darkness below.

Lord Roger was still wrestling with the ladder. Another of his men was helping. With a tremendous effort they hurled the ladder back. It hung for a moment, as if undecided, then began to swing slowly back, until it hurtled down in a long arc. In the dim light, Peter saw three doll-like figures falling clear to the ditch sixty feet below.

A hand touched Peter. It was Robert.

'This is no place for you, my lord,' he said. 'The danger is over, now, thanks to the Lord Roger.'

Peter thankfully escaped from the frightful scene, and made his way to the solar. The Lady Marian was there, with little Henry.

'Have you killed any Welshmen, Peter?' Henry demanded eagerly.

Peter shook his head, and dropped into the window seat. He was dazed and horrified. There was still a terrific uproar from outside, and once the wall shook under the impact of a great rock hurled from a mangonel.

'Wish I was old enough to fight,' Henry continued. 'When I become a squire, I'm going to fight with the king in France. I shall get knighted on the battlefield.'

Peter looked at him, and some faint flicker of memory shot through his head. It was something the vicar had said, a long time ago. The last of the de Blois family, Sir Henry de Blois, was killed at the battle of Poitiers. Yes, that was it.

He groaned, and hid his face in his hands. The Lady Marian glanced across at him.

'You are cold and tired, Peter,' she said in her soft voice. 'Come and sit by the fire. Here is some mulled wine. It will do you good.'

Peter moved over gratefully, and sipped the steaming drink. It was hot, and he felt new life flow into his tired body. From outside, the din died down, and then silence fell. The door was pushed open, and Lord Roger stamped in, tugging at his bascinet.

'Aha!' His eyes fell on the wine, and the food on the table. 'Some venison, Marian. I am starving.'

He sat down, and picked up a hunk of cold meat. He bit into it with his strong white teeth.

'Have you killed lots of Welshmen, Father?' Henry enquired hopefully.

'Hundreds of them, Henry,' Lord Roger said cheerfully. 'You can have two of them for breakfast.'

'No, thank you, Father,' Henry said politely. 'I would rather have some eggs.'

Lord Roger chuckled, and drained the tankard of wine.

'Have you pushed them back from the walls, sir?' Peter asked.

'Yes, and they have lost many men, too.'

'What will they do next?'

'Attack in the morning. With a battering ram, I expect.'
Lord Roger frowned. 'But it is those cursed trebuchets
that are doing the damage. We must get word to William
de Chaworth.'

'How?' Peter sat up. Lord Roger sounded worried.

'I don't know. But we will see in the morning. Now, to
bed, all of you.'

There were no more alarms that night, and when Peter
had finished his breakfast the next morning he went up on
to the walls. The ditch where the fight had taken place was
filled with a mass of rocks and earth. But the Welsh were
not in much evidence. They had drawn well out of range.

'What next, William?' Roger asked.

The old soldier shrugged his shoulders.

'A battering ram and a tortoise, if I was out there,' he
said.

Lord Roger nodded, and Peter tried to remember his
lessons. A tortoise was a long wooden shelter, carried over
the battering ram, so as to protect the men swinging the
ram. It did not sound a very effective weapon with which
to batter down the immensely thick walls. But as William
pointed out to Peter, the ram was used to make a breach in
the wall, and so dislodge sufficient stones to bring down a
larger section of it.

Maelgwyn might have heard William's advice, for half
an hour later there were signs of another move from the
enemy. Rough shelters of brushwood were rushed
forward to within arrow-range of the walls. The Welsh
archers crouched behind these, and opened up a rapid fire
on the defenders above.

'What are they bringing up now?' Lord Roger asked,
peering over the parapet.

'A ram!' exclaimed William.

A long procession of men were walking quickly
towards the wall, under cover of the fire from their

archers. They were carrying a long pole with an iron-tipped head: the ram itself.

As they neared the wall, a long wooden shelter, built with sloping roof, was brought forward, and put over the heads of the men on the ram. This would keep off arrows, and any stones thrown from above. The clumsy tortoise then advanced slowly over the flattened ditch.

The pace of the fight rose to a tremendous pitch whilst all this was going on. Despite the covering fire from the Welsh, the garrison of the castle was massing above the threatened point on the walls. A heavy return fire was being hurled at the archers, and already big stones were crashing down on the tortoise.

'Wait!' Lord Roger shouted. He turned an exultant face to William. 'Maelgwyn has made one mistake, William,' he said.

Old William chuckled and nodded. 'Yes, my lord. Fire?'

'Yes, and haste, William. When I give the word.'

William rushed off, and as Peter watched him give rapid orders which sent men of the garrison scurrying here and there, he wondered what the significance of the word 'fire' could be.

The tortoise was at the foot of the walls now. A series of dull thuds showed that it was already at work, despite the hail of fire from above.

'Ready, my lord,' shouted William from his position right over the top of the tortoise.

A group of men was gathered round him, holding great buckets, from which smoke was rising.

Lord Roger waved his arm. Instantly a fresh hail of objects fell on the tortoise, burning fragments of wood, smouldering rags, lime, and anything that would burn.

For a moment nothing happened. Then one of the baulks of the tortoise roof broke into a sheet of flame as the men on the wall hurled down torches on the highly combustible stuff below. In a flash the flames spread, and the whole length of the tortoise was a blazing mass.

The unfortunate men underneath broke and ran. As they did so, the whole castle garrison sprang into action. A rain of arrows shot down, followed by rocks, boulders, and any missile they could lay hands on. The Welsh ran in all directions, squealing like a herd of pigs, as they fell in waves under that withering and merciless fire.

Peter put his hands up to his eyes, and stumbled away, feeling sick with the sight of these fresh horrors.

'That will cool Maelgwyn's blood,' Lord Roger remarked with satisfaction.

But the casualties on the defenders' side were serious too. The fire from the Welsh bowmen had been horribly accurate, and the giant trebuchets were once more coming into action.

Lord Roger's face lengthened as he received a report of the situation from William. Many of the animals in the courtyard were being killed by the flying stones, and that meant that the food supply would be cut down in the event of a long siege. Casualties on the walls were heavy. The mangonels, which were now keeping up a heavy fire on one section of the wall, were causing serious damage, and it was unlikely that Maelgwyn, if he used a ram again, would make the same mistake. Next time, he would cover the roof of the tortoise with leather hides which would be soaked in water, and stop any danger of fire.

Peter listened to the conversation. The situation was by no means desperate. The castle could hold out with ease for the next three days; even if the Welsh breached the walls at one point, there was still no guarantee that they could force their way in then. And the water supply was intact.

'But I should feel happier if Sir William knew what was happening,' Lord Roger said.

He leant on the parapet, and stared over to the blue hills in the distance. At that moment, William came running up. His face was drawn with worry.

'They are digging a mine, my lord,' he said.

'Impossible!' Lord Roger snapped. 'There is solid rock under the curtain wall on this side.'

William leant forward, so that only Lord Roger and Peter could hear his words.

'But there is one spot, my lord,' he said.

Lord Roger stiffened, and he stared at William with consternation.

'But I warrant that no one knows of that except you and I,' he said quickly.

William nodded, and then cocked a thumb in the direction of the Welsh lines.

'That young Welsh chieftain,' he said grimly. 'He was often walking round the ditch. He might have . . .'

Lord Roger's mailed hand came down with a crash on the stone parapet.

'Glyndwr!' he muttered, and his fingers curled, as if they were itching to grasp Glyndwr's neck.

'But what is it?' Peter asked.

'There is one spot under the walls where the rock falls away,' Roger said. 'They could dig a tunnel there. We have always kept it a close secret.'

They knelt down, and peered over the walls. The Welsh were digging a zigzag trench towards the wall. From the shelter of that they would start to burrow underground. By the next morning, if all went well with their tunnel, a huge section of the wall would collapse, and with their superior numbers, they would rush the breach, and burst through the gap.

'We must send to Sir William,' Lord Roger said. He glanced at old William. 'But how?'

'There is one chance, my lord,' the veteran said. He hesitated, and glanced at Peter. 'You remember when the Lord Peter was lowered over the precipice after that nest, my lord?'

Lord Roger stared at William, and then shook his head. 'It is too dangerous,' he said.

Peter jumped up. The thought of going down the face of that frightful cliff was unnerving, but he felt something urging him on.

'Let me go, please,' he said.

Lord Roger's stern face softened as he looked at Peter. He dropped his hand on his shoulder.

'Very well, Peter.'

They hastened down the steps to the courtyard, and while William fetched ropes, Lord Roger led Peter to the well. They ducked their heads under the low doorway, and slowly crept down the passage cut in the solid rock. Narrow windows had been cut on the right, and these looked down the side of the cliff. It had not changed much since he had seen it last, Peter thought.

'Make for Llandarn, Peter,' Lord Roger said. 'You might find a horse in the hamlet of Roust. Then gallop as if the fiends themselves were behind you. And if you see any Welsh, give them a wide berth. If they catch you—' He broke off, and frowned.

William arrived then with coils of rope, and Peter fortunately forgot what Lord Roger had muttered about being caught by the Welsh. If he had stopped to think, he would have realized that Maelgwyn would probably hang him without mercy.

The two men fastened the rope round Peter's waist, and tied the other end to the rock window.

'We can lower you most of the way, Peter,' Lord Roger said. 'After that you will find a ledge. Follow that to the right, and then jump the rest.'

Peter nodded. His mouth was dry, and his fingers were trembling as he tested the rope.

'Ready?' Lord Roger looked down at him, and smiled. 'It will be simple, Peter.'

Peter nodded. He could not have done otherwise, even if he had wanted to. Some driving force was making him do this ridiculously risky job. He had no head for heights; the mere sight of that frightful precipice made him feel sick, and his head began to spin like a top.

'Don't look down,' Lord Roger muttered, as he and William lifted Peter through the narrow window cut in the solid rock.

Peter nodded again, and scrabbled for a grip with his feet. They began to lower him, and he looked up. Lord Roger paused, his dark eyes on Peter's face.

'God be with you, my son,' he said quietly.

Peter choked and blinked. This would be the last time he would see Lord Roger; he was convinced of that. He nodded once more; speech was beyond him at that moment, and then he dropped his eyes to the wall of rock on a level with his eyes.

They lowered him slowly. It was not so difficult. The cliff face was not as sheer as it appeared from a distance, and Peter was able to get a grip here and there with his feet. And as long as he did not look down! He fought against the temptation, but it was too much for him.

He glanced furtively at his feet. Below them—nothing; nothing but the face of the cliff, and far below, as if seen from an aeroplane, the trees and undergrowth at the foot of the precipice.

Peter shut his eyes. His head was reeling and there was a feeling of appalling sickness rising like a tide inside his stomach. He swayed dangerously out from the wall. With a bump, the rope pulled him in again, and from above came a warning shout. With a tremendous effort, Peter looked up again, and saw two faces looking down at him. He had dropped an immense distance already. Not far to go.

For the next few minutes, the descent went well. And then he reached the full extent of the rope. He had to look down now, to find the ledge. Yes, there it was. A narrow ridge, just wide enough for a foothold, and he could hold on with his hands at the rough surface of the wall. He edged towards the ledge, and seizing a sturdy bush with one hand, untied the rope round his waist with the other. As he let go, the rope flickered up, and had gone. He was on his own now.

The next five minutes were a blank as far as Peter was concerned, and he could never remember exactly what did happen. He had a faint impression of scrambling slowly down that dreadful ledge, his hands gripping the wall desperately, and the skin ripping from his fingers as he went; foot by foot he sidled to the left, and down and down he went.

How long he had been, or how far he had gone, he had no idea. His breath was coming in agonized gasps; he was at the end of his tether. His legs felt like lead, and were trembling uncontrollably with the strain. His shoulders were aching almost beyond endurance, and his frightened brain was telling him that he must let go at any moment.

And then he did let go. Peter swayed outwards, made a final convulsive effort to regain his balance, and fell.

'This is the end,' he thought, and then a violent shuddering blow struck him. He felt something tear at his clothes, his face was slashed viciously by thorns, and he was lying on the ground, gasping and sobbing.

He opened his eyes, for he had closed them instinctively as he fell. He was lying on the soft grass at the foot of the cliff, and with a shout, he jumped to his feet. But a feeling

Peter was able to get a grip here and there with his feet

(See page 169)

of nausea swept over him, and staggering against the side of the cliff, he was violently sick.

As the spasms died away, he felt better. He looked up, and shut his eyes again. Surely he had not come down that frightful precipice? Two tiny dots were sticking out from the wall far above. It was Lord Roger and William. He could see them waving, and he waved back.

The gesture made him pull himself together. He had got so far, and he must not let them down now. Wiping away the streak of blood from his face where he had torn himself on the thorns he broke into a trot. As he went, he glanced down at his clothes. His hose were ripped to shreds, but his mail shirt had saved him from worse cuts and bruises, and his steel helmet had probably saved his life when he fell those last few yards.

He left the cliff behind, and came out on a rough sheep track. He knew where he was now, for he had ridden this way with Henry last week. It would take him to the little hamlet of Roust, part of Lord Roger's estates, where he might find a horse.

At the end of ten minutes, Peter was breathless, and nearly exhausted; but the village was in sight. He slowed down to a walk, and as he breasted a slight rise, dropped to the ground and peered through a bush at the squalid huts just ahead. But there were no Welsh in sight. Two men were working on a plot of cultivated ground behind one of the miserable huts.

He jumped to his feet, and went towards them. They saw him coming, and stood there perfectly still.

Peter searched their faces desperately for some sign of friendship. For after all, as he knew, they were of Welsh blood, too, and might be glad of the chance to change masters. With a sigh of relief he recognized one of the men. He was a fellow called Dilwyn, who had suffered from a poisoned hand. He had come to the castle for treatment, and the Lady Marian had cured him with some ointment of her own making. Surely the man would be grateful for that, Peter hoped.

'My Lord Peter!' gasped Dilwyn.

'I want a horse, Dilwyn, quickly,' Peter said.

'There are no horses here, my lord. The Welsh took them all.'

Peter groaned. He was exhausted now, and he could never cover the distance to Llandarn on foot.

'But there is a pony here, my lord,' Dilwyn said. 'He was too small to be of any use to them.'

'That will do,' Peter said, almost crying out in his relief. 'Anything, but quick!'

They took him to one of the huts, and produced a small mountain pony. He was not an impressive sight, compared to the magnificent horses that Peter was accustomed to ride from the castle stables, but at that moment the pony looked a gift from heaven.

He waited impatiently while they saddled the pony, and then throwing the two men some coins from his purse, kicked his heels into the pony's side, and cantered off.

The breeze cooled his cheeks and flushed face, and for the first time since he had started on that appalling drop down the cliff, Peter began to think clearly again. His most urgent and essential task was to avoid any roving bands of Welshmen. There were certain to be plenty about, for they would be combing the countryside for food, as the Lord Roger had warned him. And if he were caught . . . But he tried not to think of that.

His pony trotted up a hill, and he saw the road stretching out ahead. It was deserted. He kicked the pony's side, and laughed. He was safe and clear. In an hour he would see William de Chaworth, and the rest would be simple, once that great soldier and fighter took charge of the situation.

For half an hour Peter rode through the deserted
countryside. He was feeling stronger every minute, and
was enjoying the ride. And then with a sickening jolt,
down went all his dreams of an easy task. For he heard the
clip clop of hooves behind him and, turning in his saddle,
saw a small group of horsemen riding furiously after him.

His heart seemed to stop. With a half-stifled cry of fear,
he crouched low in the saddle, and urged the wretched
little pony to increase its speed. But despite Peter's frantic
efforts the unfortunate animal was incapable of anything
more than a slow canter. So he pressed on, at what seemed
a snail's pace, with one eye cocked over his shoulder,
unhappily aware that the men were only five hundred
yards behind, and that they were gaining on him at every
stride.

Oh, for one of my horses from the castle, Peter gasped.
But it was no use crying for the impossible now. He
would be caught at the end of another mile. He kicked his
pony furiously, and the poor beast made one more effort.
They were climbing now, for the road was like a
switchback. Down they dropped the other side, and
ahead was another slope. It was these constant hills that
were wearing the pony down, for the better horses behind
were gaining rapidly at every hill.

They had pulled up tremendously on that last hill, Peter
saw as he threw a hurried glance behind. He crouched
lower, and shouted hoarsely at his pony as they went for
the next slope. It could not last much longer, he realized.
The pony was failing quickly now, and was beginning to
stagger. It needed all Peter's skill to keep him going at all.
They breasted the slope, and Peter raised his head.

There, a few hundred yards ahead, was the most
glorious sight he had ever seen. He stood up in his saddle,
waved his hands, and yelled like a demented being, so
great was his relief.

17

PETER RETURNS

The road ahead was filled with troops, marching steadily towards Peter. At the head was a detachment of mounted men, fully armoured, the sun flashing on their mail and plate, the devices on their shields, and picking out the colours of the pennons waving over their heads. And there was no mistake about the devices, either. Even at that distance, Peter could distinguish the black martlets of the de Chaworths.

A horseman spurred forward as Peter came down the hill, and raced up to him. From behind, Peter heard shouts, and the drumming of hooves. He looked back, and caught a glimpse of the Welshmen disappearing over the hill.

'Peter de Blois,' shouted the approaching rider in surprise. It was John de Chaworth. He gazed open-mouthed at Peter's appearance, the congealed blood on his face, his torn hose, the scratched mail, and the steel helmet.

'What is it, Peter?' He jumped off his horse, and just caught Peter in time as he toppled sideways in his saddle.

'Carreg Cennen . . . the Welsh . . . mining,' gasped Peter.

Now that it was all over, the reaction had set in, and he felt unutterably tired. His voice seemed to come from far away, and John's kindly face wavered in front of him like a badly focused film.

'What is this?' demanded a loud voice. It was Sir William.

Peter struggled to control himself.

'The Welsh are besieging Carreg Cennen, sir,' he said. 'They are digging a mine under the walls!'

'So that is where Maelgwyn has gone,' William said. Clearly Peter's information had not caused him much surprise or worry.

'But they are digging a mine!' Peter protested.

'Well, that will not cause much damage at Carreg, Peter,' Sir William said soothingly. 'It is solid rock there.'

'But they have found the one spot where there's no rock, sir, and they have mangonels and trebuchets.'

'Trebuchets!' William started. 'That is different. Quick, boy, tell me what has happened.'

Peter described the course of the siege up to the time he had left. They listened with interest, with a running commentary by Sir William on the tactics employed by either side.

'But how did you get away, Peter?' John asked curiously.

'Down the precipice.'

'What!' They stared at him in amazement.

Sir William leant down and patted Peter on the shoulder.

'You have done well, boy,' he said. 'I would not have gone down that cliff for all the gold in the Marches.'

'Peter, you're a braver man than I am,' John said emphatically.

Peter flushed, and changed the subject hurriedly.

'Will you go to Carreg now, sir?' he asked. 'They may have dug under the walls by this time.'

Sir William shook his head.

'Plenty of time, Peter. I have some experience of mining, and it will take them until dark at least. And besides, I have not enough men to tackle Maelgwyn. I have but twenty mounted men, and fifty archers.'

Peter's hopes fell with a sickening jolt.

'But we are marching to meet Brian de Camville,' Sir William went on. 'So on, and the faster the better.'

He signalled to one of his men, and Peter was given a better mount than the poor pony which had reached the end of its tether after the ride from Roust. Five minutes later, Peter was riding by John's side on the road along which he had ridden so frantically.

He gathered that they had planned to meet the force from Llanstephan, the home of the Camvilles, the previous day, when news had reached Sir William that the Welsh had broken out. Gilbert de Chaworth had made the plans from Kidwelly, after consultation with the Earl of Gloucester, the head of the Clare family, and the greatest of the Marcher Lords. It was fortunate that the Kidwelly tournament had brought them all together, for in those days of slow communications, they would have taken a week at least to concentrate their forces.

They waited an hour at the spot where the meeting was to take place. Peter fretted impatiently. But John and his father soothed him down. Carreg, as they pointed out, was one of the most impregnable fortresses in the Marches. He nodded gloomily. But the hunk of cold meat which John pressed on him, and the flagon of weak wine, did more to raise his spirits.

A shout from the sentries posted by Sir William at last announced that the Camvilles were arriving, and within a few minutes they came in sight. Peter recognized young Alain de Camville, who had been at the Kidwelly tournament, and by his side was the thick-set figure of Sir Brian.

The two leaders discussed the position. They were both experienced soldiers, and were not going to make a wild and risky dash for Carreg until they had worked out a plan. For they were still out-numbered by the Welsh, though they had the great advantage of having a solid squadron of heavily armed and mounted men, which was more than Maelgwyn had. His chief arm was the longbow, and both Sir William and Sir Brian had a healthy respect for that weapon.

Eventually they set off, the lions of the de Camvilles floating side by side with the martlets of the Chaworths. On the way, John explained the plan. They hoped to come out in the rear of the Welsh, and charge through, making the most of their mounted men, and before Maelgwyn could draw up his archers in position.

'Nearly there.' Peter raised his head. He had been drooping in his saddle, but at the remark from John, he sat up expectantly, and his tiredness seemed to drift away.

Sir William went forward to review the position, and they all waited eagerly for his report.

'They are attacking the gatehouse,' he said, 'but it does not look a serious business — a feint perhaps. Maelgwyn is massing his men for a bigger rush at the centre of the curtain wall. He may have dug faster than we thought. But it is a wonderful chance for us. What do you say, Brian?'

'I leave it in your hands, William.'

'Good! Then we form up, my men on the right, and yours on the left. Sound the trumpets, and charge right home! And God be with us!'

The attacking forces were soon drawn up, making use until the last possible moment of the brow of the hill, so that they would burst like a thunderbolt on the unsuspecting Welsh. The archers were given the task of covering fire, and attending to the Welsh longbowmen, who were the most dangerous part of the Welsh forces.

From the other side of the hill could be heard the roar of the attack on the castle. Peter fidgeted restlessly in his saddle. If they wasted any more time, they would be too late to save Carreg Cennen, he felt, and he glanced impatiently towards Sir William.

That experienced fighter was adjusting the grip of his shield, and showed no signs of hurry. But John had noticed Peter's impatience.

'The more they are engaged with the castle, the more chance we have of charging right into their midst, Peter,' he whispered.

Peter nodded. There was sense enough in that, but it did not make the waiting any easier.

Then Sir William pulled down his visor, and rode forward, turning to face his force.

He was a magnificent and inspiring figure, and a ripple of excitement ran through the ranks, as he sat there, glancing along the lines. Then he twitched his reins, turned, and moved slowly over the brow of the hill. With a clank of armour, his men followed until they were all drawn up in full view of the castle.

Peter rose eagerly in his stirrups, and gazed anxiously at it. The great walls were still intact, and the pennon of the Gauntlet flew defiantly from the gatehouse. A dense mass of Welsh were mustering in the ditch at the spot where it had been levelled, and scaling ladders were being erected against the walls. Peter caught a glimpse of steel-clad figures on the lofty parapet, and he guessed that the Lord Roger would be there, waiting for the attackers to climb up.

Then the trumpets blared, harsh, menacing and exultant, with a sound that made Peter's blood race. Sir William raised his lance, and then crouched low in his saddle, as he urged his horse into a gallop. A roar of cheers went up from the ranks behind him and they, too, moved forward, gathering speed down the slope, until the drum of the horses' hooves rose to a deep thunderous roar, mingled with the clash of armour, and the shouts of the riders.

From Sir William came a bellow of 'A Chaworth! A Chaworth!' He was riding a steady ten paces in front, his massive figure low in the saddle, his cyclas fluttering in the wind, and his long steel-tipped lance held as rigidly as if fixed in a vice.

Peter kept his position just behind John de Chaworth. What fears he might have had were thrust aside by the wild excitement of that charge, as they thundered down upon the Welsh.

The surprise was complete. There were no men posted to watch the rear, and the bulk of the archers were stationed in front of the castle. A few mounted men swung round to face the rush, but they might as well have tried to hold back the tide.

Peter had a brief glimpse of Sir William dashing like a thunderbolt at Maelgwyn. His lance caught the Welsh chief full on the helmet, and tore it off his head, as he was hurled from the saddle, and dashed to the ground. Sir William's lance had splintered at the impact, and as he pulled out his long sword, another Welshman swung at him viciously. It was a slight figure, despite the armour, and Peter recognized the coat of arms on the shield. It was Glyndwr.

Sir William swerved aside. The blow missed him, and with the same beautifully controlled movement, he struck hard with his sword. Glyndwr threw up his hands, swayed in the saddle, and toppled slowly to the ground.

But Peter saw no more of Glyndwr; he was in the thick of the fighting himself, and a Welshman rode at him from the right. He was too excited and flushed with the wild fury of the charge to feel afraid, and he guarded instinctively with his sword. His enemy slashed down viciously; the blow slithered off his sword, and he thrust back desperately. But Peter's reach was too short. And with a sudden thrill of fear, he saw the man's sword swing up again. There was a shout from behind, a figure thrust past him, his lance aimed at the Welshman's head.

'Behind me, Peter,' shouted a voice. It was young Alain de Camville.

His lance caught the enemy flush on his helmet, and he was thrown violently from his saddle as Alain rushed on, with Peter close at his heels.

But the first stage of the battle was already finished. As Sir William had planned and hoped, that surprise attack, backed by the weight and tremendous dash of his heavily armed men, had broken clean through to the castle. And the Lord Roger, as experienced a soldier as Sir William, knew exactly what to do now.

The drawbridge creaked down, and the heavy gates beneath the gatehouse swung open. Lord Roger, followed by a troop of mounted men, galloped across the ditch.

One concerted blow now, and before the Welsh could reorganize, might finish the battle, and Roger knew it. He had left his archers on the walls, from where they could pour down a covering fire, and distract the attention of the Welsh longbowmen, the most dangerous part of Maelgwyn's force.

Peter rode up to the gatehouse with Alain. As he did so, the Lord Roger pulled up his horse by Sir William's side. He caught sight of Peter, and his grim face relaxed. His gauntleted hand patted Peter on the shoulder, and he smiled down at him.

'Good, Peter,' was all he said, but it was enough for Peter.

'One more charge, Roger, and we have them,' Sir William said. 'I think Maelgwyn is down.'

'No, there he is, William,' Sir Brian said. 'Now, Roger, before he rallies them.'

The trumpets sounded shrilly, and the ranks of the Marcher Lords were re-formed. There was a pause, one more blast from the trumpets, and every lance came down as the horses moved forward, slowly at first, and then breaking smoothly into a gallop as they pounded down the steep slope.

Peter fell in behind John de Chaworth and Alain. Just ahead he could see the three knights, crouched low in their saddles, only the tips of their helmets showing above the shields.

As the pace increased Peter felt the cool air play on his flushed face, and he heard himself shouting loudly with the others. What he was saying, he did not know or care. He only knew that this was the supreme moment of his life. Never again, he was sure, would he ever feel this exultant sensation of wild excitement.

And then the first lines met. Above the shouts of rage, fear and defiance, and the steady drum of hooves, rang the clash and clangour of sword on sword. It was as if several hundred blacksmiths were hammering away like fiends on their anvils.

Peter was well protected this time, with John on one side, and Alain on the other. There was little he could do except keep his horse under control, and watch for danger. Then they were through the line of mounted Welsh. The strongest part of that line had been smashed by the three knights as they hacked their way through. Peter had a brief glimpse of Sir William as he swept a man from his saddle, and he saw the Lord Roger's distinctive bascinet as Roger drove his lance full at another Welshman. The lance splintered, and out came Lord Roger's long sword.

Another Welshman rode at him from the side. Roger swung his horse round with magnificent skill. His sword flickered through the man's guard, and he rolled from his saddle with a scream.

Lord Roger waved his sword exultantly, stood up in his stirrups and turning his head to the men behind, beckoned them on with one brief inspiring flourish. Then he settled down again in his saddle, and side by side with the other two knights, rode furiously at the last remaining Welshmen.

To Peter, the battle was over. For they were opposed now by a long line of footmen. They could not possibly stand up against that charge of the Marcher cavalry, he thought.

But those Welsh footmen were the longbowmen, an arm that was destined a few years later to change the whole tactics of fighting, as they were to show in the great battles in France under King Edward. And Lord Roger, Sir William, and Sir Brian, born and brought up in the Welsh Marches, knew only too well the possibilities of the longbow, with its high rate of fire, its amazing accuracy, and the frightful power of penetration of the steel-tipped shaft.

There was only one thing to do. And that was to charge home with desperate speed, and before the archers had a chance to fire more than one volley.

They were just in time. Maelgwyn was trying to rally his men. But he was too late. One volley they fired, and that was the end. But it was an effective fire, for all that. The arrows clinked up against the armour of the Marcher force, brought more than one man crashing to the ground, and killed many horses.

Peter saw Lord Roger's horse swerve violently, and then rise in the air, his fore-feet pawing furiously. Then he toppled sideways and Roger was flung clear.

With a strangled cry, Peter spurred his horse forward, and ahead of his two protectors. Lord Roger was on one knee, his shield held over his head. Standing over him was the short powerful figure of Maelgwyn, and in his hand was a thick stumpy mace. He brought it down with a crash on Lord Roger's shield with a vicious force that made Peter gulp. Lord Roger rolled over, the shield dropping to the ground, and Maelgwyn stepped forward for the kill, his mace swinging back for the final blow.

Peter flung himself from his saddle, and darted forward, sword outstretched. Instinctively remembering old William's lessons, he slid forward his right foot and thrust for the throat, the vulnerable part where the armour was weakest.

The point of his sword hit Maelgwyn full on his *coif de maille*. He rocked on his feet, and his mace crashed down, just missing Lord Roger. Then he turned on Peter, and swung back the ponderous mace with both hands.

Peter flung up his sword to ward off that dreadful blow. He saw the mace fall, slowly at first, then with ever-increasing speed. He was aware of a figure rushing forward on his left, and heard a warning shout in Lord Roger's well-known voice from his right.

Then a smashing weight crashed down on his helmet. He felt the ground hit his shoulder as he fell, and then he rolled over. The grass was damp and cool against his face. A voice was shouting, 'Peter, Peter!' and then it faded away. Peter's ears were filled with a dull roaring noise that rose to a high-pitched shriek. There was a red glare in front of his eyes.

He groaned, and shut his eyes. And then the mists closed swiftly over him.

He slid forward his right foot and thrust for the throat

(See page 184)

18

Peter Finds his Proof

Peter groaned again and opened his eyes. There was still a loud roaring in his ears, and he felt sleepy, and half dazed. As he moved, he rolled over, and found himself staring up at the deep blue of the sky.

A single-engined aeroplane was banking steeply, just overhead, its powerful engine filling the whole valley with a furious high-pitched roar. Then it straightened, and darted off, and the sound changed to a steady drone, dying away into the distance.

An aeroplane, Peter thought drowsily. Probably from . . . He sat up quickly. An aeroplane! What on earth could an aeroplane be doing at the siege of Carreg Cennen?

He was sprawling at the bottom of a ditch. To his right was the hard white surface of the main road. Peter leapt to his feet, and thrust his head through the gap in the hedge.

But there was nothing to be seen there. Carreg Cennen stood solidly on its pinnacle of rock; daylight showed through the gaps in its grey walls; strands of ivy crawled up the shattered towers of the gatehouse. No pennon fluttered from the battlement; no steel helmets flashed in the sunlight on the walls.

With a smothered groan, Peter stared down at the green fields below him. But they were empty. Gone were the madly charging horsemen who had plunged down the slope behind the heroic figure of William de Chaworth; gone, too, were the gaily coloured pennons of the knights, the roar of the desperate fight, the twanging of the longbows, the hiss of the shafts, and the deep thunder of the hooves.

Peter rubbed his aching eyes. He saw the blue sleeve of his school blazer, and his familiar flannel shorts, and school tie.

As he tried to control his racing thoughts, he heard the sound of a horn, and looking up, he saw a car sweep round the corner, and rush down the road towards him. As he moved slowly forward, the car stopped.

'Hullo, Peter!' Gwyn said. 'Had my tooth out! Like to have a squint at it? It's a whopper!'

Peter nodded, glancing at the grisly specimen in Gwyn's hand, and opened the door of the car.

'Sleeping in the sun, Peter?' Mr Evans asked. 'It's a lovely spot up here, isn't it?'

'Lovely, sir.'

Peter answered automatically, and as they drove down the hill listened with half his attention to Gwyn's exciting account of the operation at the dentist.

His head was aching dully, with a persistent and excruciating throb by the time they reached home. Mr Evans took one look at his white strained face, and packed him off to bed immediately after he had made him eat some soup. The thought of more food sickened Peter, and he dropped on to the comfortable bed with a sigh of relief. He felt exhausted and battered, and as he closed his eyes, the bed seemed to sway. With a groan, he rolled over, and buried his face in the pillow.

Then, mercifully, sleep came and he remembered no more. When he awoke, the sun was down, and the room was filled with shadows. Peter sat up, and swung his feet over the bed, as he glanced round for the familiar sight of stone walls and narrow slit window. But his bare feet sank into a deep pile carpet.

He sighed. It was ironical that when in Carreg Cennen he had yearned for the comfort of his former bedroom, and now was wishing that he was back in the turret room over the gatehouse.

The vicar was sitting in his favourite chair by the fireplace when Peter came into the lounge.

'Feeling better, my boy?' he asked, busily stuffing his pipe with tobacco.

'Yes, thank you, sir.' Peter slipped into a chair. He refused the offer of supper from Mr Evans, and listened with only half his attention to the conversation between the two men. After a while, Mr Evans turned to him.

'Hope you didn't catch cold this morning, Peter,' he said.

Gwyn chuckled. 'You must have slept for a jolly long time,' he said. 'Didn't you wake up until we came along?'

'I woke up before that,' Peter said slowly. 'I found myself holding the Gauntlet.'

There was a short silence. The vicar, who had struck a match, stared at Peter's white face until the flame of his match scorched his fingers. He hurled it into the fire with a muttered exclamation.

'And what happened then, Peter?' he asked quietly.

Peter shook his head distractedly. 'I don't know how to start, Vicar. I found myself back in the fourteenth century.'

'What!' came three simultaneous exclamations.

'Now, Peter,' said the vicar, trying to control the eagerness in his voice. 'Tell us exactly what happened.'

'Well,' Peter said slowly, trying to gather his confused and reeling thoughts, 'I was standing by the side of the road, and I had medieval clothes on. Then a horseman came round the corner. He was wearing armour, just like Roger de Blois on the brass in the church.' He paused, and his face flushed with sudden excitement.

'Oh, I know now why that brass to Peter de Blois was put up! Vicar, was Carreg Cennen ever besieged by the Welsh?'

'Several times, Peter.'

'By a man called Maelgwyn?'

The vicar started, and then nodded.

'Yes, in 1326.'

'What happened? Did he capture the castle? Did he —'

'No,' interrupted the vicar, cutting in calmly on Peter's barked questions. 'The castle was relieved after a short siege, and Maelgwyn was killed.'

'That's right!' shouted Peter. 'I saw him knocked down by Sir William de Chaworth!'

'You saw . . .?' Mr Evans glanced at the vicar with a worried expression on his face.

'Now, Peter,' the vicar said again. 'Start at the beginning, and tell us what happened.'

Peter nodded, and plunged into his story. He described the interior of the castle, the life led there, the hawking, the visit to Valle Crucis, his lessons in archery, the joust at Kidwelly, the siege of Carreg Cennen and his escape down the cliff, and the charge of Sir William and the relieving force, and the last desperate fight below the castle.

They listened to him in silence. Even Mr Evans, who looked as if he thought that Peter was seriously ill, forgot his fears in his fascinated interest. The vicar never moved. His eyes were fixed unblinkingly on Peter, and Gwyn crouched on the rug in front of the fire.

'So you see,' Peter said, as he finished the incredible story, 'I couldn't possibly have dreamt all that, could I, Vicar? How else could I have learnt about hawking, what Valle Crucis looked like; I could take you over it all. And Kidwelly Castle; I've never been there in my life. I know exactly how they dressed, what they ate, in the fourteenth

century, the rules of jousting, the meanings of coats of
arms . . .'

He broke off, and gazed appealingly at his audience.

'You do believe me, don't you, Vicar?' he asked.

The vicar nodded, and sank back into his chair. He
stared at the dark beams of the ceiling, and sighed deeply.

'You've spent the last two weeks with your nose buried
in books, haven't you, Peter?' he asked quietly. 'And I've
lent you some, too.'

Peter nodded. 'But, Vicar — '

'Exactly, Peter,' went on the vicar. 'You have soaked
yourself in medieval life. All the information you have
given us could have come from those books, you know,
my boy.'

Peter shook his head helplessly. The vicar turned, and
pulled out a thick volume from the shelf by his side. The
binding was a faded reddish colour.

'Now, take this one, Peter. Clark's *Medieval Military
Architecture*. You've looked at it?'

Peter nodded in silence, as the vicar flipped over the
pages.

'Now, you say you haven't been to Kidwelly Castle.
But you might have seen that,' and he passed over the
book.

It was open at the chapter on Kidwelly Castle; there was
a very detailed plan of the whole castle, and on the next
page a series of drawings of the vast fortress, taken from
various angles. It had not suffered greatly from the passing
of several centuries, and all the walls and towers of the
inner ward were intact.

'Yes, I suppose I might have read that,' Peter admitted.
'But what about the siege of Carreg Cennen? The
trebuchets, the mangonels, and the way they attacked
the castle? That's not in that book.'

'No, it's not, Peter.' The vicar dropped the book on the floor and pulled out a thinner volume in faded blue. 'Look at this one,' he said. '*Military Architecture in England in the Middle Ages*, by Thomson.'

He turned the pages, and looked up again at Peter.

'There's this chapter on the "Progress of Attack and Defence". Look! Here's a picture of a battering ram, with a penthouse over it, and mantlets for the archers. And on page seventy-five, a beautifully clear diagram of a trebuchet.'

Peter ran his fingers through his hair. The vicar was horribly convincing.

'Perhaps, sir,' he muttered. 'But what about the Marcher Lords, and Gilbert de Chaworth, and Maelgwyn, for instance?'

Mr Evans took a hand in the conversation.

'You might have read Oman's book on castles,' he said. 'Here it is.' He turned the pages of the brown-coloured book, filled with many photographs. 'Did you see this?'

'Oh, yes,' Peter said. 'That was one of my favourites.'

'Well, here's an account of Maelgwyn's rising.'

They spread out in front of Peter the various books he had spent so many wet afternoons poring over; there were pictures of medieval dress, details of the meals of those days, drawings of rooms, halls, kitchens, falcons and hawking, until Peter's head began to ache again.

'And the vicar took us over Valle Crucis,' Gwyn said.

'Yes, I know.' Another thought suddenly came to Peter. 'But why was the abbot exactly like the vicar, and Gwyn the same as Glyndwr?'

'Quite natural, Peter,' the vicar said. 'You would have associated us with the people of your dreams.'

'Oh, yes, I suppose so.'

Peter listened to them as they found more explanations.

'But, heraldry,' he said, interrupting. 'I don't remember seeing that in any of these books.'

Gwyn, who was hoping to find something that would help Peter, brightened up at the remark.

'I say, let's try Peter out,' he said, and snatched up a letter lying on the table. At the top was a red coat of arms.

'Whose arms are those, Peter?' he said eagerly.

Peter saw the three red chevrons, which had floated so proudly over the lists at Kidwelly.

'Oh, those are the de Clare arms,' he said immediately.

Gwyn's freckled face dropped.

'Afraid not, Peter,' he said. 'They're the arms of Cardiff.'

The vicar chuckled, and shook his head.

'Peter is quite right, Gwyn,' he said. 'So are you. The Clare arms are the three chevrons, and as they were Lords of Glamorgan, and lived at Cardiff, the city adopted their arms.'

'But how did Peter get it right, then?'

The vicar rubbed his chin with his pipe stem, and then smiled in triumph.

'Your father was at Cambridge, wasn't he, Peter?' he asked.

'Yes, sir.'

'What college?'

Peter grinned, and nodded. 'Clare College, sir.'

'I thought so. The college was founded by one of the Clare family, and they use the Clare coat of arms, of course.'

'Yes, I suppose that's right,' Peter said. 'Daddy has a cigarette box with the college arms on it.'

It was soon after that that the vicar announced his intention of going home.

'And you go to bed, my boy,' he added to Peter. 'Don't let this business worry you.'

Peter went obediently to bed. He was not worrying, as the vicar and Mr Evans had feared, but he was still unshaken by the explanation they had given him. He tumbled into bed, grinning as he snuggled down on the modern mattress, switched off the bed-lamp over his head, and fell asleep.

He and Gwyn decided to go down to the village the next morning. Peter was anxious to see the church once more, and as they walked up the nave, they saw the vicar in one of the transepts.

Peter made straight for the small brass of Peter de Blois. His curious dread of it had vanished now, and he inspected the details of the figure with rapt interest. It was a badly worn brass, though, and Peter could do little more than pick out the vague details of the fourteenth-century dress, the cote-hardie and hose which had become so familiar to him.

He turned away with a sigh. The morning sun was streaming in through the transept window, and falling gently on the tomb of Roger de Blois. It was very quiet and peaceful there; Peter felt his eyes grow moist as he bent over the chipped stonework. Lord Roger had been lying there for many hundreds of years now, under that massive block of stone. But he could not have wished for a lovelier resting place, Peter thought, and he would have been pleased to know that his tomb was still looked after with respect and care, although his castle of Carreg Cennen was nothing more than a picturesque ruin, a curiosity for passing motorists as they hurried to the coast.

Peter ran his eyes over the brass, and smiled as he saw the familiar outline of Lord Roger's armour, his cyclas, the great sword, and . . . there was something missing. Of course, Peter said to himself, there's no misericorde, Lord Roger always . . .

He gaped open-mouthed at the brass, and then swung round to the vicar.

'The dagger!' he shouted. 'The dagger!'

'What is it, Peter?' The vicar looked at him with alarm.

'I knew no one would believe me,' Peter said, 'so I buried my dagger in the bank outside the gatehouse. I can show you exactly where I hid it. It was three days ago, just before Maelgwyn attacked the castle.'

'Three days ago,' echoed the vicar. He shook his head.

'But I did!' Peter said. 'Oh, please believe me, Vicar. Can't you drive me up to the castle now? I marked the spot. It won't take a minute.'

Ten minutes later Peter was rushing up the steep slope to the gatehouse of Carreg Cennen.

'Wait a minute,' Gwyn shouted. 'Must have something to dig with.'

But Peter was too impatient to wait. He would tear the soft earth up with his fingers, if necessary. The dagger was only a few inches deep.

'Whereabouts, Peter?' queried the vicar, as he joined Peter.

But Peter was staring with horror at the tumbled mass of stones and rocks. All traces of the Lady Marian's herb garden had vanished long ago, of course. Trees had grown where neat bushes and shrubs had once stood.

'Better start digging in a straight line along here,' Gwyn said, producing a small garden trowel.

Peter nodded, snatched the trowel, and started to throw up the earth with desperate speed. At the end of five minutes he had cut a shallow trench stretching for about ten yards. But there was no sign of the dagger.

He bit his lips, and turned a despairing glance on the vicar.

'It is here, sir,' he said, 'I KNOW it is.'

'All right, Peter,' the vicar said soothingly. 'We've got plenty of time. I'll light a pipe, and sit down. It's a lovely morning, and this is one of my favourite spots for a rest.'

Peter set his teeth, and hurled himself at the trench once more. It was quite obvious that the vicar did not believe a word of his story about the dagger, but was too kind-hearted to say so.

The old gentleman smoked placidly while Peter, and then Gwyn, attacked the earth. They had ripped up a considerable stretch of turf now, and there was still no sign of anything remotely resembling a medieval dagger. Gwyn turned up some stones, but Peter hurled them over the edge of the cliff with grunts of disgust. The perspiration was streaming down his forehead, but he still went on digging with dogged persistence.

Suddenly a wild cry rang out, and the vicar jumped round. Peter was holding some object in his hand. But as he looked down at it, his expression of triumph changed swiftly.

'No good,' he said. His voice was low, and half choked with disappointment.

'Let me see, Peter.'

The vicar took the object, glanced at it, stared at Peter, and then back at the object with an odd expression on his face.

He muttered some words under his breath, and Peter looked up sharply, new hope welling up.

But nothing could have looked less like the beautiful little dagger he had buried a few days before. The vicar was holding a short dirt-covered object, and was scraping it gingerly with the blade of his pocket knife. There was metal under the encrusted earth, for Peter could see the green colour where the metal had corroded.

'But is that a dagger, sir?' he whispered.

'I think so, Peter.' The vicar went on scraping gently.

'But it couldn't have got like that in three days.'

'Three days?' The vicar smiled. 'This, my dear boy, is a medieval misericorde, which has been under the ground for at least six hundred years!'

Peter took the dagger, and tried to find some familiar detail. But it was impossible. The initials he had carved had vanished. The sharp point in which he had taken so much pride, had snapped off short. The beautifully chased work on the hilt had become blurred; the blade was green and pitted with age.

'But I was right, you see, Vicar,' he said. 'This proves it wasn't a dream. How could I have known that a dagger was buried there?'

The vicar shook his head.

'I can't tell you, my dear boy,' he said slowly. 'You may be quite right. There are more things in heaven and earth . . . ' and he shook his head again over his favourite quotation and looked down at his pipe, which he was twisting round in his fingers.

Peter was lost in thought, as he gazed at the dagger. He lifted his eyes to the towering bulk of the ruined gatehouse above. But there was no answer to his query there. He could see a large gap in the walls of his room; an untidy pile of stones lay in the arch of the gate through which the Lord Roger de Blois had been wont to ride in all the glory of his armour. The deep ditch had long since fallen in, and only a faint depression in the ground showed where it had once stood. The hands of time had pulled down the great walls, and swept into oblivion the hundreds of people who had lived on that spot.

Where were they all now? Peter wondered dully. Their bones must have crumbled into dust in the quiet churchyard of Llanferon. It was six hundred years since the banner of the Gauntlet had fluttered from the gatehouse, or the Lady Marian had ridden out to hawk by the side of her lord, to gallop over the heath, and fly their falcons.

Or was it really so long ago as that? Peter fingered the dagger. Had he really dreamt that fantastic story? Was it just by chance that he had discovered a dagger? There must be many relics left buried near an ancient building such as Carreg Cennen.

He sighed, and started to follow the vicar and Gwyn down the winding track to the spot where the car was parked.

Behind him, perched in solitary grandeur, Carreg Cennen gazed placidly across the valley to the hills, as it had done for the last six centuries, and as it would most certainly stand for many hundreds of years to come.